The adventure so far . . .

In *The Wild Women of Lake Anna,* Bailey Fish is sent from Florida by her traveling mother to live with her grandmother, Sugar, in Central Virginia. A nasty neighbor is out to get Sugar, and his son, Justin, bullies Bailey.

Sugar isn't afraid because she comes from a family of daring wild women. She tells Bailey about them, and Bailey wants to become one, too.

No Sisters Sisters Club

A Bailey Fish Adventure

No Sisters
Sisters Club

A Bailey Fish Adventure

Linda Salisbury

**Drawings by
Christopher Grotke**

Tabby House

Cover illustration and design: Lewis Agrell
Author's photo: Ann Henderson
Illustrator's photo: Paul Collins, courtesy of
MuseArts, Inc.

Library of Congress Cataloging in Publication

Salisbury, Linda G. (Linda Grotke).
    No sisters Sisters Club : a Bailey Fish adventure /
Linda Salisbury : drawings by Christopher Grotke.
    p. cm.
    Summary: After a surprise visit from the father and
half sister she has never met, eleven-year-old Bailey needs
her grandmother's help to come to terms with her con-
fused feelings.
    ISBN-13: 978-1-881539-40-7
    [1. Grandmothers--Fiction. 2. Sisters--Fiction. 3. Fa-
thers and daughters--Fiction. 4. Interpersonal relations--
Fiction.] Christopher A., ill. II. Title.
    PZ7.S1524No 2005
    {Fic]--dc22   2005048596

Also in the series:
The Wild Women of Lake Anna

www.BaileyFishAdventures.com
http://BaileyFishAdventureBooks.blogspot.com

For classrom quantity discount contact Tabby House.

Tabby House
P. O. Box 544, Mineral, VA 23117
(540) 894-8868

Contents

1

Strangers at the Door

Bailey Fish pushed the screen door open with her foot as she stepped out into the early spring sunshine. She had a shiny red apple in her right hand and her grandmother's copy of *The Emerald City of Oz* in her left.

Her kittens, Shadow and Sallie, squeezed out behind her before the wood-frame door squeaked closed. A few minutes earlier, as Bailey finished eating a bowl of oatmeal, Sugar said, "Looks like a great day for an adventure! But first I have to pay bills. Do you want to ask Emily to come along?"

"Sure," said Bailey. Her grandmother's adventures could be anything from seeing where an unfamiliar road went to stopping at a yard sale. Sometimes they went to a state park, the mountains, or out in Sugar's boat to explore

Lake Anna. Bailey enjoyed not knowing where they were going or what they might find or see. Sugar called it a "treasure hunt" when they looked for bargains. Today would be one of those days. Bailey dialed her best Virginia friend, Emily Dover.

Emily said, "I can be ready in about an hour. I have to pick up my clothes first and help Mom with the dishes."

"Sweet," said Bailey. "This will be so much fun. Sugar said we'll have lunch someplace."

Bailey was really pleased that Emily was coming. They had become good friends since Bailey had moved in with Sugar.

While her grandmother was busy at her desk piled high with papers and books, Bailey decided to read more about Dorothy's return to Oz. Until she arrived in Central Virginia, Bailey did not know that there was a series of books about the Land of Oz. Although she had seen the movie *The Wizard of Oz* a zillion times, she had not read the book itself.

Bailey often felt like Dorothy as she tried to adjust to this strange new place. Virginia wasn't Oz, but it sure wasn't at all like her former home in Florida. As Bailey became more comfortable in Sugar's house and made new friends at school, she felt less homesick.

She found a sunny spot on the gray wooden steps that needed a fresh coat of paint. There was a hint of feathery green in the tall trees surrounding Sugar's house in the woods near the lake. Bailey unzipped her dark green windbreaker halfway, turned to page 107 and pulled out her bookmark. It was a postcard from her mother in Costa Rica with a picture of a howler monkey on it.

Bailey polished the apple on her jeans as she read:

> Just as they reached the porch the front door opened and a little girl stood before them. She appeared to be about the same age as Dorothy . . .

The little girl, smiling sweetly, was Miss Cuttenclip, who lived in a paper village.

Just then Bailey was startled by the sound of the front doorbell. Nobody ever rang the bell except delivery people with packages. Sugar's friends just hollered, "Anybody home?" and walked right in without waiting for an answer. As the bell rang a second time Bailey heard Sugar shout, "Just a minute, I'm coming."

Bailey returned to the story.

> . . . here was a real girl, of flesh and blood. She was very dainty and pretty as she stood there welcoming them.

Bailey looked up and saw Sallie and Shadow stalking a skinny daddy longlegs as it moved warily along the porch floor. Sallie reached out a black-and-white paw to touch it.

As Bailey took a big crunching bite of cold apple, she heard Sugar open the creaking screen door. "Bailey," she said. Her voice sounded serious and worried.

Bailey was curious. "Who's here?"

"Some people to see us. Come inside," said Sugar, as she quickly disappeared into the house.

Bailey put down the book and apple, gathered up her kittens and followed her.

Standing in the front hall next to the grandfather clock were the strangers: a man about Sugar's height, and a girl about Bailey's age.

"Hi, Bailey," said the man, looking at Sugar and then back to Bailey. Everyone was quiet. He shifted on his feet then took a step toward her. "I guess there is no other way to say this. I'm your dad," he said.

Bailey froze and squeezed Shadow so tightly that the gray kitten yelped. She couldn't think of a word to say.

The man cleared his throat and smiled. He said, "Bailey, come give me a hug. You are as pretty as I thought you would be."

Her dad? How could this be? Her real father left home before she was born and she had never seen a picture of him even though he supposedly visited her once when she was a baby. Whenever Bailey tried imagine him, *her dad* certainly didn't look like *this* man with light-brown, very short hair, a pointy beard, hazel eyes, and a bulky, almost-black leather jacket. *Her dad* was tall, with dark curly hair and dark brown eyes. She imagined him wearing a blue denim shirt that was faded and soft from many washings.

"Come on," the man persisted. "Really, I won't bite."

Bailey's body was as stiff as a Barbie doll.

"Don't force her, Paul," she heard her grandmother saying. "This is a very big surprise, you know. Please, have a seat."

The man looked disappointed, like he had expected a different reaction from Bailey.

"We haven't finished the introductions," he said, as they walked into the living room. "Bailey, this is Norma Jean, your half sister."

He sprawled awkwardly in Sugar's favorite chair, and the girl settled into the couch and crossed her legs. Bailey didn't move from the hall. Sugar stepped behind her and wrapped her arms around her.

Bailey still hadn't taken a step. A sister? Nobody had ever told her that she had a sister, half or any other kind.

And this girl didn't look anything like her. Norma Jean had shiny straight black hair below her shoulders. Her skin was a creamy tan and she had dark, almost black, almond-shaped eyes, and absolutely perfect white teeth on the top and bottom. She was wearing a light-blue jogging suit and an ivory long-sleeve T-shirt with a palm tree hand painted in the center. Suddenly, Bailey felt out of place with her old jeans and jacket and her uncombed hair.

Bailey had straight, medium-brown hair that she often pushed behind her ears, hazel eyes and a few freckles that appeared in the summer when she had been out in the sun. Her skin was pale by comparison to this girl.

Bailey felt like she was in the middle of a dream, and not a very good one.

Norma Jean looked much too happy. "Hi, Sister," she said.

Bailey forced a "hi."

Sugar said, "Paul, I think we need to talk. Bailey, why don't you take Norma Jean upstairs to see your room."

Still clutching her squirmy kittens, Bailey nodded at Norma Jean and went up the stairs.

2

Annoying Guest

"Are you mad at me?" asked Norma Jean. "You haven't said anything."

Bailey said, "Not mad. Surprised." She leaned against the wall and watched the girl.

"Wow! You have an awesome room," said Norma Jean, hopping on Bailey's bed to see how well it bounced. "Can I play with your kittens?" she asked. "I have a cat named Kee and my brother has a dog named Kimo."

"A brother?" asked Bailey. "You're kidding!" The surprises just kept coming.

"Actually, two," said Norma Jean, taking Bailey's brush from the top of her dresser to fix her too-perfect hair.

"Paul Jr. is eight and Samson—we call him Sammy—is four. I'm ten and Dad says you're eleven." She put the brush back and held

Bailey's favorite Florida seashell necklace around her neck.

"Leave my stuff alone," Bailey said sharply.

Norma Jean just flashed a big grin, which showed all her teeth. "So now you've got a big family," she said as she arranged Bailey's cat statues, lotion bottles and pictures by height on top of the dresser. Then she picked up the picture of Bailey's mother, Molly, and the one of Bailey's former cat, Barker.

"I mean it! Don't touch my stuff," said Bailey. She didn't intend to sound upset, but she was.

"Sorry," said Norma Jean. "I didn't think you'd mind. I'm always helping my mom straighten up. She can't wait for you to come live with us now that your mother has gone away."

"What are you talking about?" asked Bailey. She had never felt so panicky in her life, like she had been shoved in a dark closet.

"Dad and I are in the States on business. We live in Guam, you know. Dad's in the Navy and we've been in a lot of countries. Have you lived anywhere else?"

Bailey said, "No, just Florida with Mom. But she's still my mom even though I live with Sugar right now. Then she's going to come home and we'll live in Florida again."

"Well, I don't know about that," said Norma Jean. "Hey, where am I going to sleep? My dad says that he wants me to stay with you for a few weeks so we can get to know each other and then you will be coming home with us so you can get to know your other family."

Bailey said loudly, "This is crazy! I'm not going anywhere with you, and this is my room. Go away. Leave me alone!"

She walked to the dormer window and looked out at the trees. Her eyes were stinging. It hadn't been very long since she had moved in with Sugar, and now this. She hated this girl and the man who might try to take her away from her grandmother.

"I'm just telling what Dad says," Norma Jean said sweetly. "Can I hold your cat?"

Before Bailey could say no, Norma Jean had Sallie on her lap, and to make matters worse, Sallie was purring.

3

Reassuring Talk

Bailey came down the stairs with Norma Jean close behind her, and headed for the kitchen. They could hear Sugar and the man speaking low and fast to each other at the table. Sugar had fixed mugs of coffee, and he was stirring milk into his.

"How do I get her to like me?" Bailey heard him ask Sugar. "Bailey looks at me like I'm from outer space."

"In a way you are," Sugar said, running her fingers through her short, dyed-brown hair. "You've got to give her time to sort all this out."

"I think once the girls get to know each other, she'll accept me," he said. "I hope so. That's my plan."

He had taken off his jacket and put it neatly over the back of a kitchen chair. Bailey noticed anchor and heart tattoos on his right arm. When Paul Fish saw her come into the kitchen, he smiled and said, "So, you girls hitting it off? I knew you would."

Bailey ignored him and touched Sugar on the arm. She whispered, "We need to talk."

Sugar said, "Paul, help yourself to blueberry muffins. Norma Jean, I poured juice for you. The glass is on the counter. We'll be right back."

As soon as Bailey closed the door to Sugar's office, her grandmother held her tightly and said, "This is quite a shock isn't it? I had no idea they were coming."

Bailey nodded. "Awful," she said, holding back a sob that felt like it was about to explode.

"Norma Jean says she is going to stay here for a couple of weeks and then they will take me back to some place where they live—Gum."

"Guam," corrected Sugar. "Look at me," she said, pulling Bailey's chin up from where it was buried in her faded blue sweatshirt. "Listen to me very carefully. You are not going anywhere. I am your guardian while your mother is traveling. I won't let anyone take you away."

"But how did he know where to find us?" asked Bailey.

Sugar said, "Paul told me he stays in touch with friends that your mother and he had when they were married. So when he found out that she was going to be in Costa Rica for a long time, he decided to try to get to know you. He *is* your father," said Sugar.

"No, he's not!" said Bailey, surprised at how angry her words sounded. "I don't have anybody but you and Mom. Besides I hate that girl. How can she be my sister?"

Sugar said, "The half means that you share the same father but have different mothers. I know this is very, very hard for you, and for me, too, but they are your family. Maybe we should get acquainted while they are in the United States."

"Did you know about them?" asked Bailey. "And Paulie and Sam?"

"No. Your mother suspected that after the divorce Paul remarried and started another family overseas. But after all these years, I was quite astonished to see him at my door. He said he was afraid to call ahead in case we said no to the visit."

Sugar paused to give Bailey a chance to think. Then she continued, "Paul and I have been talking. If it is okay with you, he would like to have Norma Jean stay here for a week so that you girls can get to know each other. First impressions are not always good ones and you might find that you have more in common with her than you think."

"I don't like her."

"I know," said Sugar. "You don't have to make a decision right now. We can talk more, then let them know in a few days. It will be up to you."

Bailey sat down in Sugar's desk chair, and pushed paperclips around with a pencil. She thought for a while. Sugar *had* promised her that she wouldn't go away with them.

"I guess she can visit," said Bailey slowly, "but she can't stay in my room. And she can't touch my things. And I don't have to like her."

"Okay. We'll figure things out," said her grandmother, giving her another big hug. "Now, don't worry."

"Will Mom be mad that he came?"

"I really don't know. I'll deal with that," said Sugar.

4

Reluctant Invitation

When Sugar and Bailey returned to the kitchen, they saw that Paul Fish had spread photographs on the table. Norma Jean was in the living room petting both kittens.

"Norma Jean said she told you about your half brothers. Would you like to see their pictures?" he asked.

Bailey had to admit that she was curious.

"Here's Paulie." The dark-haired boy was riding a bike. "And this is Sam." Sam had lighter hair than Paul—he looked more like their father than did his brother or sister. Norma Jean, the boys and their mother, Flora, were in another picture. Flora, a native of the Philippines, was smiling and hugging her children. Like Bailey's mom, Molly, this woman had dark hair. Molly's was thick and wavy, but this woman had long, straight hair, more like Norma Jean's. Flora's skin looked tan, like her daughter's.

"See, there's Kee and Kimo," said Norma Jean. Bailey hadn't heard her come in the room. The girl put her arms around the man's neck. He turned his head and gave her a kiss.

For a moment Bailey wondered what it would be like to have a real dad, and what a beard would feel like if you were touching it with your cheek.

"Well," said Sugar, "Bailey and I have been talking."

For a second Norma Jean looked a little afraid of what her new sister might say.

"And while seeing you today was quite unexpected, we think it would be okay for Norma Jean to come back sometime for a short visit," said Sugar.

Norma Jean was overjoyed. "Yippee!"

"We'll have some adventures," Sugar said with a smile in the direction of both girls. Bailey thought the smile looked less cheerful than her usual big one.

Bailey suddenly remembered that she and Sugar were supposed to go somewhere today on a special treasure hunt and now it was almost too late.

"Isn't it time? . . . Emily's waiting," she whispered to Sugar.

Her grandmother waved her hand as if to shush her.

Paul Fish said, "Sounds like we've interrupted your plans for today. I suppose we had better be on our way. You have my cell phone number. Kiddo and I will be on the road awhile. We need to visit my parents—it's been a long time, much too long, since they last saw her. And I have some business to take care of. Then we'll be back."

Sugar said firmly, and so that both girls could hear, "Paul, I need to make it clear that Bailey will not be going home with you after that. We have summer plans, and it's even possible that Molly will be here for a visit."

"Okay, okay. Maybe I can get a hug from my long-lost daughter the next time," he said, winking at Bailey. "We have a lot of catching up to do. I'm probably as nervous about this as you are. And you must have a lot of questions for me."

He held out his hand. Bailey hesitated, then shook it. She had questions all right, but at the moment, she didn't care if she ever saw her father and Norma Jean again.

5

Trying to Forget

Before Paul Fish and Norma Jean had fastened their seat belts in their blue rental car, Bailey put on her jacket.

"Let's go," she said to Sugar. She wanted to forget about these new people and have fun, like she and Sugar planned for that morning. Emily must be wondering what had happened to them. It was almost time for lunch.

What would she say to Emily? Her friend with the dark curly hair would probably be able to tell that something wasn't just right. She would ask a million questions, and then tell everyone at school.

Sugar, too, sounded like she wanted to get back to normal.

"After we pick up Emily, and get the mail in Mineral, we'll go to Charlottesville. We'll look at yard sales and consignment shops for another porch rocker. I think each of us needs one now that the weather is turning nice," said Sugar.

Bailey liked the yellow dandelions and what Sugar called "wild mustard" springing out of the ditches along the road. The air was still crisp and fresh, but the sun was warm when you were in it. On a day like today she didn't need her heaviest jacket and gloves—just her windbreaker over her favorite lavender sweatshirt.

The sunlight caught the white dogwood blossoms, and made the redbud trees look as pink as cotton candy. The thought of cotton candy made Bailey realize that she was hungry. She hoped Sugar would find a place to eat before they drove the entire distance.

Suddenly she remembered something Sugar said when her father and Norma Jean were still in the kitchen.

"Is Mom really coming home to see me?"

Sugar pushed her glasses higher on her nose, like she always did when she was going to say something important. "Molly hinted that she might, at least for a few days. But we won't know for sure until she makes plans, and that could be at the very last minute."

"I hope so. She'll like Shadow and Sallie," said Bailey, imagining how her mother would fix her hair in French braids, and they could all go on a picnic.

"But we need to get ready for Norma Jean, even though she will be here only for a short time," said Sugar.

"Where is she going to sleep?" asked Bailey, as they neared Emily's house.

"That's up to you. We can fix up the extra bedroom—it just has boxes in it—or we could put a cot in your room."

"I told you, not my room," said Bailey, with a scowl. She remembered how Norma Jean touched and moved everything. And, the memory of her petting Sallie while sitting on her bed stuck in her head.

"That's fine. You can help me move boxes to the attic and straighten things up. It won't be easy to have Norma Jean visit," said Sugar, glancing at Bailey. "And it may not be easy for her, even though she appears self-confident. She's younger than you and far from home. You know how that feels. We need to make her feel welcome, even if you don't like her."

Bailey glumly twisted her hair as she stared out the window.

6

Emily Doesn't Get It

Emily took one look at Bailey's face and said, "What's the matter?" She hadn't been in the car two seconds.

At first Bailey wasn't going to say anything, but it was bound to come out. Emily would see that the other bedroom was being fixed up and it would be pretty hard to hide Norma Jean when she came back, even though Bailey already wanted to.

"Sorry we're late. We had company," said Bailey.

"Really? Who?" asked Emily, fastening her seat belt.

"People," said Bailey, looking out the window.

"What people?" said Emily as she unzipped her blue fleece jacket in the warm pickup truck.

Bailey could tell that Sugar was listening to their conversation as she drove. Suddenly she felt like laughing.

"It was my father and . . . my half . . . half, my . . . half sister." She was giggling so hard that Sugar started laughing, too, and so did Emily, although she was not sure why.

"Your father and your half sister?" said Emily, barely able to talk between bursts of laughter. "I didn't know you had one."

"I didn't either," said Bailey, trying to stop. "That's what's so funny. And two half . . . brothers." She doubled up. "My cheeks hurt from laughing," she said, unable to get her giggles under control.

"So what are they like? What are their names?" asked Emily

"Paul Fish and Norma Jean, Paulie and Sam," said Bailey, gasping for breath. "Paul's my father . . ." and the giggles came again. "I really don't know what they are like. They weren't here very long. Norma Jean is coming back for a visit."

Emily stopped laughing and said, "That's neat. I can't wait to meet her."

Bailey remembered that it really wasn't funny. She didn't say anything. Instead of laughing, she felt like crying.

"We could have a party and a sleepover, and she can come to my house and do lots of things," said Emily. "Are you going to show her the attic and Mae's hat?"

Bailey hadn't considered doing any of that, such as letting Norma Jean see her treasures in Sugar's attic—especially her great–great aunt Mae's hat. Mae the spy. Mae, one of the family's wild women who had great adventures.

"I don't think she'll be here very long, and I don't know if Norma Jean likes parties. She probably doesn't. She's from another country. I don't think they have parties and sleepovers there," said Bailey.

Sugar turned to give her a look, but Bailey pretended not to see it.

"Then we can surprise her with one," said Emily. "I think it will be fun. She'll love it here, and maybe she will want to stay."

Bailey hadn't thought of that either.

"I doubt that she'll like Virginia," said Bailey. "It's not like Guam."

"You are so lucky," said Emily.

Sugar interrupted, "Here's a place we can get good sandwiches. Then I think we'll find an adventure up the road a bit."

7

Going, Going, Gone

"I wish my dad would take me to more fun yard sales, but he just likes to look at tools and motors," said Emily. "Mom always says we don't need more junk." She and Bailey had purchased three books for twenty-five cents each at the first stop.

"We like looking," said Bailey. "Sugar's teaching me how to dicker and bargain."

"We are going to do something new in a few minutes," said Sugar. "Keep your eyes out for signs to an auction. It starts at one o'clock."

"I've never been to an auction," said Emily.

"Me neither," said Bailey.

Within a few miles they spotted the first red sign, directing them to turn on Yanceyville Road. The signs led down a long drive to where cars and pickups were parked in a large field.

Sugar said, "First, we need to register at that trailer, and get our number. Then we'll walk around to see what is being sold. If we want to buy something, we have to get in on the bidding, unless the price gets too high. Sometimes you can get a bargain, sometimes not. If we can't find anything here, there are always other auctions and yard sales."

The three of them walked together, with the girls squeezing between farmers in bib overalls and women in jeans and denim jackets to look at what was for sale. Sugar stopped to talk to friends from the historical society.

"Go ahead and look around," she told the girls. "I'll meet you by the auctioneer's platform when the bidding starts."

Bailey and Emily wondered if all the boxes, furniture, books, dishes, and garden tools had come from just one house. There seemed to be lots of stuff. They looked at old dolls, toy tractors, a typewriter, and a plastic flamingo.

"Mom would like that," said Bailey.

Then, over near the auctioneer's stand were three rocking chairs. The smallest looked like it might be just the right size for Bailey. She tried sitting in it.

"This would be perfect," she said to Emily. "I could paint it."

"Do you have any money?" asked Emily.

"I have $20 from Mom. Let's show Sugar."

Her grandmother was still talking when the girls found her. Bailey knew she shouldn't interrupt, but she was afraid the auction would start and she might not be able to bid on the chair. She cleared her throat a couple of times, hoping to get Sugar's attention.

Just then, the auctioneer called for the first item. The crowd moved closer to see what was on the block. Sugar said, "I think if we head for the tree, we will be able to see better."

"Sugar, I saw a rocker," said Bailey. "I've got $20."

"Then, bid on it," said her grandmother.

"Me?" asked Bailey, surprised.

"By all means. I'll be right next to you as an advisor."

Bailey's heart pounded.

The auctioneer was a lanky man—tall and thin like the Oz scarecrow, decided Bailey. He wore a black NASCAR cap, and kept the microphone so close to his mouth it looked like he was about to eat it.

He tried to interest the crowd in a potbelly stove. "Who'll give me $200," he began. He sold a chain saw, a china cabinet, bedroom set, and large mirror. Next were boxes filled with odds and ends. Nobody seemed to care what they were buying because they were so inexpensive.

Then came a hammock, gas grill, picnic table, high chair, and the first two rockers. Each of the chairs went for more than $20. Bailey was discouraged.

The auctioneer's helper put the one she wanted on the platform.

"Needs work, and it's more of a lady's chair," he said, "but this would be nice on a porch on a warm summer day."

Bailey wished he would stop trying to talk other people into buying it.

"Who'll give me $10?"

Bailey was ready to hold up her hand, but Sugar said, "Wait."

When he couldn't get the bidding started at $10, he chanted, "Five gimme five," and Sugar said, "Go!"

Bailey held up their number, 162.

"I'm bid five, who'll gimme seven? Five dollar bid, now five. Gimme seven."

A man's hand shot up.

"I'm bid seven, now got seven. Will ya give me nine? Gimme nine."

Bailey held up 162 and the auctioneer continued his fast talking.

"I'm bid nine. Will ya gimme eleven?"

The man lifted his hand.

Emily said, "Oh, no!"

"I'm bid eleven. Got eleven. Gimme thirteen," said the auctioneer.

Up went 162.

"I need fifteen for this pretty chair. Who'll give me fifteen?" He looked around.

The other bidder's hand went up again.

Bailey couldn't stand it. "I'll give you $20," she shouted. "That's all I have."

The auctioneer laughed, and looked at the other bidder. He shook his head no.

"Going once. Going twice. Sold to 162," said the auctioneer, and he banged his gavel.

Emily grabbed Bailey and gave her a big hug.

Sugar said, "You did a fine job. What color are you going to paint it?"

"Purple," said Bailey, "my mom's favorite color."

"We'll get a can of paint in town," said Sugar, as they strapped the chair into the truck.

8

Checking E-mail

After Sugar and Bailey dropped off Emily and returned home from the auction, Bailey finally remembered her apple and book. The apple had turned brown where she had taken a bite that morning, so she tossed it as far as she could in the woods for the deer.

Because the air was cooler in late afternoon, she brought her book back inside. But before settling in a comfy living room chair to resume reading, Bailey turned on Sugar's computer to check for e-mail. It was unlikely that there would be one from her mother. Molly was traveling deep within the Selva Verde rain forest. She was doing more interviews and research for her big magazine article. Molly was only able to e-mail Bailey when she returned to the lodge near Volcano Arenal.

Earlier in the week Bailey received a message from her best Florida friend, Amber. It was all about boys, especially Ritchie Mossbagger.

Amber wrote that he was really cute. Bailey laughed when Amber said that Ritchie "accidentally on purpose" bumped into her in the lunchroom and then offered to give her a chocolate chip cookie his mother made. He blushed when his friends teased him saying, "Ritchie loves Amber. Ritchie loves Amber."

Amber said she hoped she would see him at one of the summer camps, but his family might be going to Maine for a month.

Bailey saw that Amber had written again:

From: <jbs25@yermail.net>
To: "Bailey"<baileyfish@gmail.com>
Sent: 4:32 p.m.
Subject: Ritchie M.

Hey Bailey. Ritchie asked me to go to the movies. His mother won't let us go alone so she's going too. She says she'll sit in the back. Yeah, sure. Mrs. Mossbagger will probably sneak up behind us. Love, Amber

Bailey grinned. She remembered Mrs. Mossbagger from band parent meetings. She was loud and always in charge of everything and tried to get her mother, Molly, to help make holiday ornaments to raise money for the band.

Molly told her she didn't have time but would write a check instead. Bailey was relieved because her mother wasn't very good at making things and she knew that Mrs. Mossbagger would complain that they were terrible or probably not use them at all.

She typed:

From: "Bailey"<baileyfish@gmail.com>
To: <jbs25@yermail.net>
Sent: 7:06 p.m.
Subject: guess what

Dear Amber: I have a father after all and a half sister Norma Jean. She's only 10 and is coming to stay with us for a week. And two half brothers. I don't like her. My father is in the Navy and they move around a lot. I got all A's on my tests. I wish you could come visit this summer. Tell me about the movies. Best friends forever, Bailey.

After Bailey sent the e-mail she thought about writing her mother, but she wasn't sure if she should say anything about the visit from Paul Fish and Norma Jean. No, Sugar said she would bring it up. Besides, when Norma Jean went back to Guam with their father, that would be the end them.

Bailey logged off and went upstairs where Sugar was stacking items to be moved out the spare room.

"Help me move these boxes to the attic, then we'll bring down the cot. We can take my sewing material out of this dresser so Norma Jean has room for her clothes," she said.

Within thirty minutes they had cleared enough space for the little folding bed and had made it up with fresh sheets, one green plaid and the other white with yellow flowers. It never bothered Sugar that nothing matched.

In the linen closet Bailey found a light blanket, a small chenille, cream-colored bedspread, and a plump pillow that looked big for the cot.

She dusted the family pictures hanging on the walls—people from her mother's side of the family. After Sugar said, "I guess we are done for now," and went downstairs, Bailey looked around the room one more time. She remembered when she first saw the bedroom that was now hers. It looked pretty awful until she and Sugar had fixed it up to make her feel at home.

Even though Bailey didn't want Norma Jean to visit, she knew that Sugar expected her to be nice. She decided to put one of her stuffed bears—not her best one—on the big pillow.

Spending a week with Norma Jean was going to seem like forever.

9

Surprise Picture

Bailey finished three more chapters of *The Emerald City of Oz* before turning out her light. She leaned back on her extra pillows. Sallie and Shadow were on her bed, grabbing at her toes when she wiggled them underneath the blankets. It was one of their favorite nighttime activities. But lately, after she turned off the light, they found a toy or one of her hair bands and played wild games under her bed until she called them to be petted on her pillows.

She wondered where Norma Jean and their father were going and when they would come back. It was very strange having a father you didn't know you had and really didn't know, and a half sister and half brothers. Even though she tried not to think about them, they kept popping into her head.

Sugar knocked. "Still awake? I saw your light."

"Yeah," said Bailey, glad for her grandmother's company.

"May I?" asked Sugar as she sat on the edge of Bailey's bed.

Bailey nodded.

Sugar said, "A long time ago you asked if I had a picture of you and your father. I knew I had one somewhere, but you know how my house is. So I've been looking in drawers and boxes. This is what I found."

She handed a small photo album to Bailey.

"Your mother started this when she and Paul got married. She gave this little one to me and made a larger one for herself with other souvenirs, such as the wedding invitation and gift cards."

"She never showed me," said Bailey, puzzled.

"I think she got rid of hers after she and Paul were divorced. Sometimes people do that," said Sugar. "They want to put the past behind them."

Bailey held the album carefully. The silver covers were tied together with gold ribbon. She opened the first page. There was a picture of her mother and Paul all dressed up for their wedding. They both looked happy. Her mother wore a sparkling white gown and had her hair pulled up in a fancy twist, with daisies and a sprig of white baby's breath tucked in. Paul was wearing a dark suit and a red tie. He didn't have a beard, his hair was longer, and he was beaming. Another picture showed the bride and groom, and their parents.

After several pages of wedding pictures, there were snapshots of Paul and Molly on their honeymoon cruise. They looked very happy as they sat by the pool, and sunbathed at the beach on St. Thomas in the Virgin Islands. Bailey turned the pages slowly. Next were baby pictures of Bailey, and photos of Molly's first house in Florida, one that Bailey didn't remember.

The baby pictures showed Bailey in her crib, in an infant swing, eating peas in her high chair, looking at a book about farm animals, and taking a bubble bath, but her father was not in any of them.

Finally, after several blank pages, she found a loose snapshot of her father hugging baby Bailey. He looked both happy and sad.

"That was taken when he came to see you when you were just a few months old," said Sugar. "That was the picture I was looking for."

Bailey studied the snapshot. It was taken after the divorce, after his remarriage and before Norma Jean was born. Just Bailey and her father.

"Why didn't he come see me again? Didn't he love me?" she asked in a tight voice.

"I believe he wanted to spend more time with you, but things just didn't work out that way," Sugar said. "I think you need to ask your parents, because I don't have the answers."

Bailey felt just like the time when she was back in Florida at a beach. A huge wave knocked her down, and she went under. She swallowed a mouthful of saltwater, and thought she was going to drown. Another wave crashed over her and her knees scraped on sand and shells.

Her mother saw what happened, dashed into the water after her, and yanked her to safety. She pounded Bailey's back to make sure she didn't have water in her lungs, then wrapped her in a big towel and carried her to the beach blanket, even though Bailey was almost too big to be lifted.

While Bailey rinsed the salt and sand off her face with drinking water from a bottle, her mom told her how worried she was. Molly said that they would go back in the surf together in just a few minutes. "I don't want you to be afraid," she said. "You just need to learn how to jump the waves."

Until her mother left for Costa Rica, she had always been there for Bailey.

But where had her father been all this time? One picture of him. One hug in her whole life. And he didn't even come by himself this time to see her. He brought his darling Norma Jean, his other daughter, the one he called, "kiddo," who had spent her entire life with him.

"If you'd like to keep the album," said Sugar, "it really should be yours."

Bailey didn't say anything. She wrapped her arms around Sugar and held on tightly. Sugar's sweater was soft, like a baby blanket.

As soon as her grandmother left the room, Bailey placed the album in the bottom drawer of her desk, under her old school papers.

Why should I care about him? she thought.

10

Sisters Club

From: <Mollyf2@travl.net>
To: "Bailey"<baileyfish@gmail.com>
Sent: 10:50 p.m.
Subject: Your father

Dearest Bailey: I understand you have had a visit from family that we didn't know about. I don't know what to say. Your father and I haven't communicated since you were little, so I didn't know for sure where he was living. I'm annoyed that he waited until I was out of the country to try to find you, but I guess after all this time there isn't any harm. I'm curious about him. Tell me everything. Paul was a handsome fellow back when we were young. Things just didn't work out.

Sugar says you are nervous about him. That's OK. Take it slowly. It's probably best to visit with him only at Sugar's house when she's around. I wish I weren't so far away so we could talk in person, but my interviews are going very well and I think my article is going to be great. The editors already want me to do another. Love, Mom

Bailey was angry that her mother had kept information about Paul Fish a secret. She wasn't sure what to say. Should she tell her mom that she was mad at her? Did her mother even care about how she felt? She sure didn't sound like she did. Bailey decided to write nothing about them to her. After all, what would she say? How much she hated them for barging into her life with Sugar, and about how annoying Norma Jean was? So she just wrote:

From: "Bailey"<baileyfish@gmail.com>
To: <Mollyf2travl.net>
Sent: 5:32 p.m.
Subject: hiya

Hi Mom: Are you really coming home for a visit in a few months? Love, Bailey

She suspected that as usual, her mother wouldn't answer that question. She never did. To her friend, Amber, she wrote:

From: "Bailey"<baileyfish@gmail.com>
To: jbs25@yermail.net>
Sent: 5:57 p.m.
Subject: did he

Has Ritchie tried to kiss you yet? Tell me the truth. If I could pick sisters, it would not be Norma Jean. It would be you and Emily. Bailey.

Amber later replied:

From: jbs25@yourmail.net
To: "Bailey"<baileyfish@gmail.com>
Sent: 8:12 p.m.
Subject: sisters club

Let's have a Sisters Club—and just best friends
can be in it. What do you think? No, Ritchie
hasn't kissed me yet. I hope he does. His mom is
always around. Love Amber

A Sisters Club of best friends—that
sounded like a great idea. *And annoying little
sisters won't be allowed in*, thought Bailey, *even
if they are just visiting for a week.*

Bailey couldn't wait to tell Emily. At the
same time she felt a twinge of guilt. She had
never treated anyone this way before. All of
her life, everybody always told her how nice
she was to everyone. She shared her lunch if
someone forgot his. She was kind to kids who
weren't popular. But this was different. Even
though there had been many times she wished
she had a brother or sister, she hadn't wished
for Norma Jean, a genuine pest. Bailey's best
friends were her real sisters, not this person
who just showed up at the front door, grinned
too much, and couldn't keep her hands off
Bailey's special things, including her kitten,
Sallie.

11

No Sisters Sisters Club

Later that evening, Emily called Bailey about their science homework assignment. Bailey told her about Amber's idea for the Sisters Club.

"I would pick you as my sister, too," said Emily. "But I don't know if we should keep real sisters out. Nannie is only seven—too little to be in it—but Norma Jean is the right age. She might be fun."

Bailey said, "No, this is a special club, just for best friends because they are better than sisters."

"Would it just be the three of us?" Emily wondered.

"For now," said Bailey. "We'd have to vote to let anyone else in."

"We'll have to keep it a secret," said Emily.

"Uh-huh," said Bailey. She had never liked it when other kids had private clubs and kept her out, but at the moment she didn't feel very good about her feelings. The very thought of that buttinski Norma Jean, who had just plopped into her life, annoyed her. She was especially annoyed that Norma Jean seemed so happy about finding her and didn't care how she, Bailey Fish, felt. The more she thought about it, she was upset that Norma Jean knew everything about their father and Bailey knew nothing. So even if the club was not a nice thing to have, Bailey didn't feel nice.

"What will we call it?" asked Emily.

"How about the No Sisters Sisters Club?" suggested Bailey.

Emily laughed. "Let's tell Amber," she said. Then she added, "We've got to have rules, and a special password, and maybe certain clothes. We'll all wear the same colors or something."

"The next time you come over we can e-mail Amber together," said Bailey. "But remember, it's got to be a secret from everyone."

Bailey hoped Sugar would not find out about the club. She knew her grandmother would not be pleased.

Amber loved the idea. But she wanted to include one other best friend from Florida so that she would have another club member to talk with about it. She wanted to invite Heather, someone Bailey really liked from her former school.

"What's our password?" Amber wrote.

"How about Cuttenclip?" Bailey typed back.

"Huh?" wrote Amber.

"It's from an Oz book and nobody will guess it."

"I like it," said Emily.

"I think we should wear jeans and red shirts when we have meetings," wrote Bailey.

Amber e-mailed back: "I'll tell Heather."

12

Old House

Without looking, Bailey scooped a spoonful of oatmeal from her green pottery cereal bowl and put it in her mouth. She was reading on page 180 about Dorothy going on an adventure in the woods while Sugar leafed through the newspaper and finished her coffee.

> The woods are always beautiful and impressive, and if you are not worried or hungry you may enjoy them immensely.

However, Dorothy was both worried and hungry and so she was hurrying through the woods and not paying much attention to its beauties. A fork in the road led to Bunbury, a place where the houses were made out of crackers, bread sticks and bread crusts. *Funny,* Bailey thought. She was so engrossed in her book that she didn't even notice Sallie and

Shadow chasing a pink rattle-mouse under the kitchen table. The toy slid under the glass-enclosed bookcase stuffed with Sugar's well-worn cookbooks, and recipes torn from newspapers and magazines.

"The fog will lift by ten," said Sugar.

Bailey didn't answer. She kept reading about Bunbury while her hand automatically moved her spoon from bowl to mouth. She really liked the way her grandmother prepared the hot cereal with just a dash of cinnamon and a big spoonful of brown sugar that soaked in with milk.

"I think we need an adventure today," said Sugar loudly as she folded the newspaper before placing it in the recycle box.

Bailey heard that and looked up.

"What sort of an adventure?"

"A walking adventure," said Sugar. "When the fog lifts, the day will be beautiful. Warm. You'll probably want to wear jeans, your brown shoes, and a sweatshirt or jacket."

"Can we have a picnic?" asked Bailey.

"Good idea," said Sugar. "You can make your famous PB&J's."

"Deal," said Bailey, closing her book. She had a new postcard from her mother to use as a bookmark. On it was a colorful picture of a three-toed sloth. Her mom had written: "Don't be a lazy sloth. Help around the house," and added a smiley face. Bailey knew her mother was just trying to be funny. Molly was aware that Bailey was helping Sugar a lot, plus taking care of the kittens and her own things.

Just as Sugar predicted, the fog vanished by the time they were ready to leave.

"Where are we going?" asked Bailey as they clomped down the front steps.

"There is a path that leads through a pine forest, down the hill, round and about until we get there."

Bailey grinned. Wherever this place was, it was bound to be interesting.

Sugar walked briskly, but stopped often to look at little plants pushing up through the moist dead leaves.

"Look, here's a fern, and this is a little laurel and there's a holly. And look at the lichen on this rock, and the shelf fungus on this branch," she said, pointing.

Bailey marveled at each discovery. Sugar seemed to see things that Bailey did not notice.

Ture-ee tur-ee

"What's that?" asked Bailey, looking up.

"Listen to that beautiful call," said Sugar.

"That's a bluebird. Watch carefully and you may see a pair."

The walk resumed. They jumped over fallen trees in the path, and ducked under low branches. In an area filled with pine trees twice as tall as Sugar's house, the ground was soft with a thick bed of pine needles. When they came to a muddy spot near a small creek, Sugar stopped again and looked at the path. "Fox tracks," she said. Bailey knelt down to have a better look.

"We have two kinds of fox in this area," said Sugar. "The gray fox with a lovely thick tail, and the smaller red fox. I've seen them at night."

"Really?" asked Bailey. "Can I see one?"

"We'll watch from the porch," said Sugar. "Sometimes the gray fox sits on a tree stump in the backyard and wraps his tail around it. And I've seen a red fox climb a tree."

Bailey said, "I didn't know they did that."

Sugar continued briskly down the path with Bailey close behind. A wiry branch snapped in Bailey's face. "Ouch," she said, rubbing her stinging nose.

The path merged with what looked like an old road. It had deep ruts on either side of a higher center mound.

Bailey looked at her watch. They had been hiking almost twenty minutes.

"We're almost there," said Sugar.

"Where?" asked Bailey.

"There," said Sugar, pointing.

Up ahead and to the left was a rundown, very old, two-story farmhouse. Clapboard siding that had once been painted white, was now as brown as the leaves under their feet. Glass was missing in three upstairs windows. Near the bolted front door, a lace curtain fluttered in a window. Bailey shivered.

"This house is near the road?" said Bailey. She was surprised to see a driveway and the street beyond.

"Yes, I like to walk through the woods, but you can also get here by car. It's actually on the next road around the bend from us."

The house looks spooky, thought Bailey.

Sugar said, "No need to be afraid. No one is inside. The place has been empty for years."

She walked closer. Bailey hesitated, then followed.

"Who lived here?" Bailey asked.

"A family by the name of Emmett," her grandmother said. "The house was built more than 150 years ago. The Emmetts farmed the area for decades. When old Mr. Emmett died, his only son wasn't interested in maintaining either the farm or the old house, so he just left them. You see a lot of abandoned houses like it around here," added Sugar.

"Didn't Mr. Emmett have any other relatives?" Bailey asked.

"Yes, his younger cousin, who is still in the area. She's very old now. The cousin has a daughter, Martha Keswick, and a grandson, Will. They both live a few hours from here. The land is now owned by Will, who plans to fix up the house and live here someday."

Sugar walked up the porch steps, testing them carefully to make sure the boards were still sturdy.

"Follow me," she said.

13

Spooky Rooms

Bailey wasn't sure she liked this adventure. The old house made her worry. What if a bear was inside? What if this Will Keswick showed up and yelled at them for going in? What if there was a rotten board and she or Sugar fell through it and became trapped? Nobody in the whole world knew where they were.

Sugar was humming. She didn't seem at all alarmed. "Don't worry. I know Will. He asked me to check on things inside from time to time to make sure nobody vandalizes the house or property. But you are never to come here without me. Promise?"

Bailey nodded.

"Why would anyone vandalize the house?"

Sugar hesitated, then said, "I know this is hard to understand, but besides the usual mischief-makers, there is a man from out of state who wants this land for development. He has tried to get Will to sell. Will refuses because he wants to fix up the place, but if the house is destroyed, Will may not care about living on the property. That's what worries me."

Sugar lifted a frayed welcome mat and picked up a key. She turned the lock and pushed the door. The house was dark, and damp from the cold.

Bailey didn't want to go in, but she was also curious.

"Look at this," said Sugar. She held up two magazines that were on a table near a sagging, overstuffed chair. "The dates are from the 1960s. That's when people might have been last living here." She blew dirt off the covers.

Sugar said, "I imagine old Mr. Emmett liked to smoke his pipe while he sat in that chair. He could see his fireplace, and snow falling outside that window."

In a corner of the living room was an upright piano with several ivory keys missing. Bailey walked over and touched middle C. It made a muffled *twang*.

Sugar said, "I've heard Mr. Emmett loved to have his younger cousin visit. She sang beautifully and played the piano for him."

From the center hall, Bailey could see many rooms, including a kitchen with a wood stove, a few cupboards with the doors wide open and a sink. She hoped Sugar wasn't planning to have their picnic at the rickety kitchen table. The cane seats on the wooden chairs didn't look strong enough to hold people, and the house still gave her the creeps.

Bailey asked, "What's that noise?" It sounded like something alive was upstairs.

"Might be an animal or a bird," said Sugar. "Let's have a look."

Before Bailey could object, Sugar was testing the safety of the steps. This time Bailey didn't follow. Then Sugar called, "Come see. It's a nest of baby vultures—as ugly as their parents."

Bailey decided to go on up.

The nest was in one of the bedrooms next to a broken window. What a racket the birds were making! Bailey stayed in the doorway. She didn't want to be there when the parents returned.

"Let's go," said Bailey, tugging on Sugar's sleeve.

"Sure," said Sugar. "There is more to see outside."

Bailey was relieved to be on the front porch again. She followed Sugar around to the back of the house where they discovered a smaller porch that led to the kitchen, and steps to the cellar. Bailey was glad that Sugar didn't want to explore down there.

Sugar stopped by the back porch steps. "Vandals, again," she muttered. "Look at this, Bailey." She pointed at three smashed wooden chairs and fresh tire tracks near them on the lawn.

"I'll have to call Will," she said. She sounded worried.

Bailey had more questions about the man who wanted to buy the property, but Sugar seemed to be finished talking.

As they walked toward the orchard, her grandmother showed her what was left of a vine-covered chicken coop, an outhouse, and a barn where Will stored building materials.

They both jumped at the sound of bicycle tires screeching. As they turned, they saw a boy and a brown dog.

"It's Justin," said Bailey. "What's he doing here?"

The dog started toward them, then stopped, as if waiting for Justin's okay.

Sugar called out, "Hey, Justin, what's up?"

"Just looking around," he said. He pushed his dark hair back under his turned-around baseball cap. He dropped his bike and shoved his hands in his pockets.

"What are you looking for?" asked Sugar.

"Nothing special. Old bottles in the woods. Stuff," he answered.

"We like to find things, too," said Sugar with a smile.

Bailey still couldn't figure out Justin. He had stopped teasing her about her name and hadn't called her Florida girl since he found out that she was a reading buddy with his little sister, Fern. And, even though they rode the same school bus, he never mentioned the time that he helped her after she twisted her ankle in the woods when she was looking for gold and trying to be a wild woman.

She didn't know if he was mad because Sugar was partly responsible for having his father arrested that night for hurting him, and for polluting Contrary Creek. Bailey still wasn't sure if she liked him even a little. Right now she wanted him to go away.

Bailey's stomach growled. "I'm hungry," she said to her grandmother.

"I know the perfect place to eat," said Sugar.

"Where?" asked Bailey, hoping it would be far away from the house.

"There," said Sugar, pointing at a cluster of gnarled fruit trees, "in Mr. Emmett's orchard. Help me roll this log over by that apple tree. It will give us something to sit on."

Sugar called, "Justin, we have an extra sandwich. You're welcome to join us for a picnic."

"No, thanks," he said, looking like he would like one. "I gotta go." He hopped on his bike, whistled for the scruffy dog and off they went.

Sugar pulled the sandwiches out of her pocket and handed one to Bailey.

It was a beautiful spot for a picnic, but Bailey felt like the Emmett family ghosts were watching from the windows as she took her first bite. She shivered again.

14

Little Graveyard

"We're going to take a different way home," said Sugar, as she finished the last piece of sandwich. "There is something else on that path that I want to show you."

Bailey took one final look at the old house, trying to imagine what it would have been like when it was in good condition and children her age played there.

She knew that Amber would be interested in the vultures. Amber would say, "Yuck!" But if she ever came to visit, Bailey knew that Amber would want Sugar to take them to the old house. Norma Jean would want to see it, too.

Norma Jean. Why was she even thinking about Norma Jean? Bailey had been trying to forget her. That girl was becoming annoying even when she wasn't around.

Sugar pushed aside brush and found the trail leading from the orchard through a small weedy pasture, and then back into the woods. They jumped across a stream, and got their shoes mucky on the other side.

Sugar took a deep breath. "I love the smell of spring," she said. "It's so fresh and earthy."

"How do you know so much about the woods?" asked Bailey.

"The wild women of this family all were, and are, observant. They like nature. My mother, your great-grandmother, would play nature games with me when we walked."

"What kind of games?" asked Bailey.

"We would see who could notice the most types of flowers, birds, trees, or bugs."

"Bugs?" asked Bailey.

"Yep. Sometimes that game was the most fun because we would have to sit very still or overturn a log, or lift up some leaves to see what might be lurking," said Sugar. "Mae was a good spy because she was an observer. In fact, all the wild women were smart because they learned how to observe and ask questions."

"Is that what you were doing at the old house?" asked Bailey, as she jumped over a branch in the path.

"We can learn a lot about people and the past. Once the old buildings are gone, they are gone for ever. I like to see buildings restored. They are often very beautiful and teach us about what life was like long ago," said Sugar. "Our next stop is the old graveyard."

"The what?"

"There are many family cemeteries in the country. This one is old and in rough shape. It's a short walk on a path that leads to my backyard," Sugar said. "Follow me. Observe!"

As an official wild woman in training, Bailey decided she needed to become a better observer. She looked carefully at the tree trunks to see the different types of bark, some rough, some smooth. She noticed that the bark on the hardwood trees, such as the oaks, was grayer than the brown bark of the pines.

"Why is the bark gone from some of the trees?" asked Bailey, pointing.

"Ah, good observation," said Sugar. "That's where the bucks rub the 'velvet' off their antlers," she said. "If you look over there you will see where the deer have pawed the ground— and piles of little dark balls. Those are the deer droppings."

"Are those deer hoof prints?" asked Bailey, excitedly.

"Go, girl!" said Sugar. "Another good observation."

 As Bailey looked farther, she saw eight small objects jutting out of the hilly ground. She ran ahead of Sugar. It was the cemetery. Sugar unzipped her tan jacket lined with red flannel and found a large rock to sit on while Bailey went from stone to stone, trying to read the names and dates.

"They are mostly little children," she said with surprise.

"Times were hard a hundred years ago. Families couldn't get the kind of medical care or immunization shots that we have today," said Sugar.

"That's really sad," said Bailey, but before she had a chance to look at all of the graves, Sugar suddenly got up.

"Oh dear," she said. "Someone has vandalized one of the headstones." She pointed to a larger one. It looked like it had been knocked over, maybe when someone threw a large rock at it. "That's terrible," said Sugar. "Look here."

Bailey saw nine beer cans, two empty cigarette packs, a torn potato chips bag, and three plastic water bottles.

"We'll report the vandalism here and at the Emmett house to Will," Sugar said. "We'll come back later with a plastic bag for the trash. I usually take one with me when I walk."

"I don't get it. Why do people make such messes?" asked Bailey.

"I don't know," said her grandmother. "Animals don't mess up the woods and roadsides like this. Just people."

"I'll help you clean up. Mom and I always picked up trash in our neighborhood," said Bailey.

"What a team we make!" said Sugar

"Trashbusters," said Bailey, with a happy smile.

"So, how did you like the woods adventure?" asked Sugar as they neared her house.

"Fun," said Bailey, "but a little spooky."

They stamped the dried mud off their shoes and left them on Sugar's back porch. Before Bailey could e-mail Amber, she heard Sugar listen to a message on the answering machine. It was from Paul Fish. He and Norma Jean would be returning soon.

Rats! thought Bailey.

15

Vandalism Worries

Sugar asked Bailey to make sure the rice didn't boil over while she called Will Keswick. She told him that she couldn't determine if kids or someone else had done the damage.

Bailey could tell that Mr. Will was upset about the vandalism to the family farm. She leaned on the counter while listening to Sugar's conversation.

"We'll go back again soon," Sugar told him. "But you should get in touch with the sheriff."

"Can he really fix up that house?" asked Bailey, once Sugar hung up the phone. "It doesn't look that good right now."

"It's an historic place," said Sugar, "and it will look terrific when Mr. Will restores it. He wants to work on it this summer. He likes living in old homes, and this one is very special because it belonged to his great-uncle. Will remembers playing there as a small boy."

Sugar looked out the window at the setting sun. She said, "What worries me is that the land is becoming valuable now. We know this developer from out of state is trying to buy up a lot of properties besides Will's, and he has no interest in local history. Those he has already purchased are falling down or 'things have happened' to them."

"Things like what?" asked Bailey.

"Oh, vandalism, and one was mysteriously burned to the ground," said Sugar.

Bailey looked worried.

"I didn't mean to alarm you," said Sugar. "I'm so used to talking out loud about these things when I lived here alone that I forget sometimes that you are a kid."

"I'm old enough to know what's going on," said Bailey.

"I know," said Sugar, patting her shoulder.

"What can we do?" asked Bailey.

"Not a lot," said Sugar, "other than to just be observant."

Bailey said, "I think the rice is done."

Sugar said, "Turn off the heat and fluff it. I need to make one more call. The number is in my office."

Bailey tried to imagine what the Emmett house would look like with new windows, fresh white paint and a modern kitchen, and especially with no vultures' nest in the bedroom. As interesting as the nest was, she didn't think that it belonged in that room if people were going to live there.

She was proud that Sugar had told her about the Emmett house, and she planned to be very observant to help protect it.

Bailey found a large fork and fluffed the steaming rice. She put the rice in a covered bowl to keep it warm until Sugar returned.

Then she remembered the message on the answering machine. Norma Jean would be coming back soon. This was not going to be fun.

16

Norma Jean Returns

From the attic window, Bailey watched the blue car come up the driveway. She saw Norma Jean and her father get out. He opened the trunk and lifted out a bright pink suitcase with wheels. They were back from their travels much sooner than expected. School wasn't even over yet. Paul Fish put a pillow under one of Norma Jean's arms and a large stuffed monkey under the other.

"Bailey. Company!" Sugar called when the doorbell rang.

She could see Shadow hiding under a chair in her room, but Sallie had already gone downstairs and Norma Jean was rubbing the kitten's chin.

"Well, here's my oldest daughter," said Paul Fish, smiling at Bailey.

"Hi," she said, shoving her hands in her pockets.

"No 'Hi, Dad'?" he asked.

"Now, Paul," said Sugar, "you promised."

"I know. I know," he said, with a sigh.

"How about something to drink?" asked Sugar, "and my slightly burned brownies?"

"I'll take a brownie with me—I really can't stay but a minute. I've got to catch my flight. But first, how about a picture of my two girls?"

Paul Fish pulled a digital camera out of his jacket pocket. "You two stand over here. Closer," he said, motioning. "Smile and say, 'stinky cheese'."

Bailey felt Norma Jean's hand creep around her waist. Bailey made her lips turn up in a faint smile, but, as always, Norma Jean grinned so big you could see all her teeth.

"Great," said Paul. "I know Flora and the boys will want to see what you look like. I'll give you a call to find out how things are going. Be good, little one," he said to Norma Jean, who gave him a long hug and kiss. "See you in a week or two, kiddo. Don't know exactly when I'll be back."

Rats, Bailey thought. That was a lot longer than she had expected. Even Sugar looked startled.

"Maybe we can get to know each other better then," he said to Bailey. He extended his hand to her. She shook it, but for a moment was afraid he was going to pull her closer for that hug she didn't want.

"C'mon, Norma Jean," she said quickly, jerking away. "Let's go up to your room."

"I'm not sleeping with you?" asked the younger girl, as she waved good-bye to their father. She sounded a little scared.

"No, we have a special room for you," said Bailey. "It's near mine."

As Norma Jean unpacked her suitcase, Bailey noticed that Sallie had settled down between the bear and the monkey on the pillow.

Great! thought Bailey. *Just great!*

"So, what are we going to do while I'm here?" asked Norma Jean. She brushed her hair into a ponytail. "I like to play games, go outside and explore, cook, draw, go for rides."

Bailey knew that she had to be nice. She had promised Sugar she would try.

"We could walk in the woods. I know where there is a cemetery. It is kind of hidden so most people don't know it is there."

"Cool!" said Norma Jean. "Who's buried there? Are you scared when it's dark?"

Bailey said, "Not really. I've never gone at night though. It seems to be for just one family—from a long time ago."

"Let's go now," said Norma Jean.

Bailey was surprised that the girl was not afraid.

"Not today," said Bailey. "It's too late." Then she said, "If you like to read, my grandmother has a ton of books in her library."

"I do like books," said Norma Jean. "I also know sign language. We learned it in school. Here's the sign for sisters." She formed Ls with her thumb and first finger, then overlapped them after she touched her right cheek.

"But mostly I like to draw. My mom says I'm going to be a great artist someday. Would you like to see pictures I drew while we were traveling?"

Before Bailey could say yes, Norma Jean pulled a sketch pad out of her suitcase and handed it to her as both girls sat on the cot.

Norma Jean didn't draw like most of the kids Bailey knew. She was really good. She made buildings, animals, and people look very real.

"You're a good artist," said Bailey as she turned the pages, and looked at the faces of a man and a woman. "Who are they?"

"Those are my grandparents—my dad's mom and dad. I guess they are your grandparents, too," she said. "I'm named after Grandmother Fish. Grandpa's name is Harley."

Bailey hadn't considered that she might have other grandparents. She was curious as she studied Norma Jean's drawing. She could see that Paul Fish resembled them. She wanted to hold the pictures up while she looked in the mirror to see if she looked like them, too, but not in front of Norma Jean.

"They asked about you," said Norma Jean. "I told them everything."

Bailey didn't want to hear about Norma Jean's visit. It didn't feel like these strangers were her grandparents. Besides, where had they been all her life? And why hadn't her mother mentioned them either? None of this made sense.

"You did a good job," interrupted Bailey, as she looked at the sketches.

"Thanks, Sis," said Norma Jean, with that irritating toothy smile. "Let's show Sugar."

17

Honorary Granddaughter

Sugar was talking on her cordless phone in the kitchen when the girls found her. "I've got it on my calendar," she said. "Put me down for a tuna casserole."

"She sure likes to talk a lot," said Norma Jean.

"She's always trying to save animals, and help the environment," said Bailey proudly. "She belongs to different groups. Sometimes I go with her to meetings."

Norma Jean picked up Sallie and walked to the refrigerator where Sugar and Bailey posted notes and photographs.

"Who is this?" asked Norma Jean, as she pulled a picture out from under its magnet.

"That's my mom," said Bailey. "Put it back. Sugar really likes that one of her."

"I'm not going to hurt it. I'm just looking. She's really pretty."

Bailey felt uneasy. "C'mon. Put it back."

"I'm just looking. Is that your Florida house?"

"Yeah."

"Nice house. Is that your cat?"

"His name was Barker."

"What happened to him?"

"He was killed by a car just after Christmas. Sugar let me get kittens when I moved here."

"Too bad about Barker," said Norma Jean. She sounded like she meant it.

Just then Sallie began to wiggle. As Norma Jean tried to hold her, she bent the picture so that it put a big crease through Molly's face.

"Oh, no!" said Bailey. "Look what you've done!"

"I didn't mean it," said Norma Jean. "Really I didn't. I'm sorry. Maybe we can flatten it out."

After Sugar put the phone in its receiver she took the photo and said, "I'm sure this was an accident, but please try to be more careful with other people's things."

"I'm really sorry," said Norma Jean.

Sallie jumped to the floor as Norma Jean threw her arms around Sugar's waist.

"I wish you were my grandmother. You're so nice," she said.

"You can be one of my honorary granddaughters," said Sugar, hugging back.

First she's trying to take my kitten, and now my grandmother, thought Bailey, with the biggest scowl of her life. *This isn't fair.*

18

Planning the Sleepover

Emily phoned Bailey six times the day after Norma Jean arrived. "When can I come over and meet her?" Emily begged. "Everybody wants to see your sister. And we need to plan the sleepover. Mom says we could have it at our house, if you want us to."

Bailey still wasn't sure she wanted anyone to meet Norma Jean.

Bailey finally whispered in the phone so Norma Jean couldn't hear, "Norma Jean is really very shy. I don't know about having a party. . . ."

She didn't realize that Sugar had come up behind her. Her grandmother tapped her on the shoulder and said, "A party to welcome Norma Jean would be nice. Tell Emily that we will have it here on Friday night."

Norma Jean yelled, "Yippee! A sleepover party!" She leaned next to the phone trying to listen to the conversation. "That's awesome."

Bailey, turned away from her and said to Emily, "I guess it will be here on Friday. I'll talk to you later."

By the time Bailey hung up, Sugar and Norma Jean were sitting at the kitchen table, and Sugar had printed Slumber Party on a large yellow pad.

"How many friends would you like to invite?" Sugar asked Bailey.

"Probably six or seven. Emily, Beth, Rosalie, Lisa, Madison, and Shaunda."

"I'll make the invitations," said Norma Jean, "and then we can give them out in school on Monday."

"You're coming to school?" asked Bailey, with a sigh. She hadn't counted on that.

Norma Jean said, "Why not? I brought some work with me. I have to write a report on what my trip was like, including going to my sister's school."

Bailey said, "But it is a long day and . . ." She tried to get Sugar's attention, but her grandmother seemed to be lost in thought.

"That's okay," said Norma Jean. "I think it will be fun. And I can meet your friends."

Sugar said, "I've got paper and colored markers for making invitations. Bailey, what do you think we should serve?"

"Pizza," interrupted Norma Jean. "That's my favorite sleepover food."

"Liver and spinach," said Bailey. She was feeling grumpy, not at all like her usual self.

"You're silly," said Norma Jean, patting Bailey on the shoulder.

"Pizza it is," said Sugar. "And we'll have salad, and maybe make popcorn. We can rent a video or two."

"I like Disney," said Norma Jean before Bailey could open her mouth.

Whose house is this anyway? Bailey wondered.

Sugar said, "Your bedroom isn't large enough for so many girls. Would you like to sleep in the living room? If so, I'll need help rearranging things."

"I don't have a sleeping bag," said Norma Jean.

As usual Sugar had just the thing. "There is an extra one in the attic. I bought it last winter at a yard sale," she said. "We can air it out before Friday. I hope you girls don't plan to stay up all night. I'm not used to missing my sleep." Then Sugar added, "And no gooey messes, like whipped cream or shaving lotion in someone's hair."

Sugar pushed her glasses up her nose, and tried to look firm. "You both look surprised that I know about such things, but believe it or not, I was once a girl, and I also remember some of the slumber parties your mother had."

"Why, what did she do?" asked Bailey

"I probably shouldn't give you any ideas," said Sugar.

"Oh, c'mon, tell us," said Bailey.

"Tell us! Tell us!" said Norma Jean.

Sugar smiled and said, "Bailey's mother, Molly, was a bit on the wild side—a wild woman even when she was a preteen. And she loved parties. When she was twelve, I told her she could invite twelve girls for supper and to spend the night. Well, fifteen girls showed up, and so did seven boys—with sleeping bags."

Bailey laughed and Norma Jean grinned.

"I said the boys could stay for hamburgers, but they had to call their mothers and go home after we ate," said Sugar. She tried to look serious but her lips were twitching.

"Then what happened?" asked Norma Jean. "Did the boys leave?"

"I had my suspicions when I heard a lot of giggling and whispering coming from Molly's room. So I went in," Sugar said, getting up from her chair to demonstrate with great exaggeration. "I tiptoed over to where the bed was pulled out from the wall. There, rolled in a blanket between the wall and the bed, was Donny Stevens. He had come back in through the window," Sugar said. "I unrolled him and together we walked to the phone, where he called his mother—again—to come pick him up."

Sugar paused, then said, "Molly claimed she didn't know a thing about it. But because I suspected more wildness, I had a second plan of action." Sugar tiptoed with giant steps back to her chair.

"What was your plan?" asked Bailey.

"When the lights were out and the girls were pretending to sleep, I unrolled my sleeping bag in the doorway. That way I would know if they were leaving to get into shaving cream or a food fight," said Sugar.

Both girls smiled at the thought.

"Did they plan a gooey fight?" asked Bailey.

"Oh my yes. But it stopped them in their tracks when I sat straight up. So beware. Sugar knows all the tricks. Now, let me get that paper so you can start working on the invitations. Bailey, what do you want written on them?"

Before Bailey could say a word, Norma Jean sketched a picture of the two of them with arms around each other, like they were best friends.

"This is the picture I'm going to draw on all the invitations," she said.

Bailey rolled her eyes at Sugar.

While Norma Jean made the invitations, Bailey excused herself and went into Sugar's office to e-mail Amber.

From: "Bailey"<baileyfish@gmail.com>
To: <jbs25@yermail.net>
Sent: 4:45 p.m.
Subject: NSSC

Cuttenclip. We've got to meet soon. She is driving me crazy. Best friends, Bailey

Amber later replied:

From: <jbs25@yourmail.net>
To: "Bailey"<baileyfish@gmail.com>
Sent: 7:35 p.m.
Subject: NSSC

Cuttenclip. Tell me when. Amber

From: "Bailey"<baileyfish@gmail.com>
To: <jbs25@yermail.net>
Sent: 7 a.m.
Subject: NSSC

Cuttenclip. Emily will be here Friday for the sleepover. We'll e-mail then. Bailey

19

Return to the Graveyard

"Let's go find the graveyard," said Norma Jean after Sugar suggested that the girls go outside after lunch for an adventure of their own.

It was a short hike through the woods to the cemetery. The girls walked through damp leaves covered with little branches that had broken off during ice storms. Norma Jean stopped frequently to look at plants and flowers growing on the forest floor.

"These are beautiful," she said. "I never saw anything like this in Guam—it's a tropical island, you know."

"I never saw anything like this in Florida either," said Bailey. "We had palm trees and palmetto. It was so thick that we really couldn't walk through the woods. And rattlesnakes."

"We have palm trees, too," said Norma Jean. "Not trees like these."

Norma Jean pulled a little notebook out of her pocket and sat down on a log. She sketched a tree that was tilted and the holly bush next to it.

Bailey wondered if they would ever get to the cemetery if Norma Jean stopped all the time.

"What's that bird?" asked Norma Jean pointing at something reddish as she stood up again.

"I really don't know," said Bailey. "Sugar can tell you. She knows all about everything."

"Are there always so many spiderwebs?" asked Norma Jean, brushing one out of her hair.

"Spiders are starting to come out now, but Sugar said there are more in the summer. Hey, we're almost there," said Bailey as she ducked down to avoid a large web.

"Oh, I see it," said Norma Jean, pushing ahead of Bailey. She counted the eight brown gravestones.

Norma Jean squatted down to read the names and dates. "Look, here is one that says

LUCILLE E.

REST WITH THE ANGELS.

"It looks like someone brushed the leaves away and placed a little ball and toy dishes next to it," said Norma Jean.

"Don't touch them," warned Bailey.

"Why not?" asked Norma Jean.

"You should never touch anything in a cemetery. It might be bad luck."

That didn't stop Norma Jean. She traced the name Lucille with her fingers and picked up the little china dishes to look at them closely.

"Put them back! Now!" said Bailey. Norma Jean could be really freaky sometimes.

"Okay. Okay. I didn't break anything," said Norma Jean. She sat on a rock and sketched the tombstones.

"Do you draw everything you see?" asked Bailey.

"It helps me remember things," said Norma Jean. "Sometimes I use little sketches later in a bigger picture. Like these might be good at Halloween."

"Ready to go back?" asked Bailey.

"What's down there?" asked Norma Jean, pointing into the woods that sloped toward Lake Anna.

"I haven't gone that way yet," said Bailey. "There isn't a path."

"We don't need a path," said Norma Jean. "We could just leave markers to show us how to get back."

"What kind of markers?"

"Sticks. Stones. It really doesn't matter so long as they point the way," said Norma Jean.

"There is an old house that way," said Bailey, pointing in a different direction. "Only we can't go there without Sugar."

"Why not?"

"It's too dangerous. And it might be haunted," said Bailey, hoping that would make Norma Jean less interested.

"I just love haunted houses," said Norma Jean. "I'll ask Sugar to take us."

Grrrrr, thought Bailey.

20

Bailey's School

"You have such beautiful hair," said Emily to Norma Jean. She was sitting behind Bailey and her sister on the bus.

"Thanks," said Norma Jean. "Sometimes my mother brushes it one hundred times, just like she does hers. I've only gotten as far as twenty-five. Then my arm gets tired."

"You live in Guam?" asked Emily.

"Yes, for now, but my dad says we might not stay there long. He wants to transfer to Puerto Rico or some place in the States." She put her arm around Bailey. Bailey pulled away. She wished Norma Jean wouldn't do that, especially in front of her friends.

"I didn't know you were going to move," said Bailey as she stared out the window at the newly plowed farmland.

"I guess he decided after we visited my grandparents," said Norma Jean. "He said it would be nice to be closer to them and to my big sister." She smiled at Bailey, who continued to look away.

"Oh, I forgot. Here's your invitation to my party," Norma Jean said to Emily.

Emily opened it carefully to make sure the tape didn't tear the paper.

"Did you draw this picture? It looks just like you and Bailey," she said.

Norma Jean beamed, then asked, "Who's that boy in the back of the bus."

Bailey and Emily turned around.

"That's Justin," said Emily, like she couldn't believe that Norma Jean would even ask about him.

"He has nice eyes," said Norma Jean.

Bailey and Emily looked at each other in amazement.

~ ~ ~

Sugar had made arrangements with the school to allow Norma Jean to attend Bailey's fifth-grade classes rather than go alone into the fourth grade with her own age group.

To Bailey's dismay, Norma Jean didn't just sit back, observe and keep her mouth shut. Each time the teachers asked a question of the class, Norma Jean's hand shot up first. And to make matters worse, she was always right.

"I like your school," said Norma Jean as they walked down the hall to the girls' room. Bailey pushed her arm away three times.

Word quickly spread that Bailey's surprise sister was visiting from overseas. They were surrounded by curious classmates when they sat down at the cafeteria table. Norma Jean was clearly enjoying the attention. She smiled happily and chatted, while Bailey sat to one side, listening, but pretending not to be interested.

Norma Jean noticed Justin eating alone three tables away. "Doesn't he ever talk?"

"Nuh-uh," said Bailey. "Not for awhile."

Norma Jean smiled and waved at him. Bailey couldn't tell if he was smiling back, but he didn't seem to be frowning quite so much.

What's the matter with her? wondered Bailey. *There are plenty of other boys to talk with besides Justin.*

Later, while her classmates were busy eating, Bailey quietly pointed out to Norma Jean the girls who would be getting invitations to the sleepover. Norma Jean delivered the folded papers very secretly so that others wouldn't feel left out.

~ ~ ~

In the band room, Norma Jean pulled up a chair next to Bailey so she could read the clarinet part.

"I play the piano and trumpet," she said in a loud whisper. "Dad says I have a natural talent for music, like he does."

Bailey didn't have to ask what he played. She knew by now that Norma Jean would tell her everything.

"He plays the clarinet, just like you," continued Norma Jean. "He plays in his own jazz band."

That was something else she hadn't known about him. Bailey didn't let on, but she was pleased that she and her father played the same instrument. Maybe he would want her to play for him when he came again. No, not until she was a lot better. He might laugh if she made a mistake, not like her mother who always clapped when Bailey finished practicing, even if her clarinet had squeaked.

Bailey opened the music folder and took out "Let There Be Peace on Earth," one of her favorite pieces. She was nervous with Norma Jean there and the music slipped to the floor.

"Maybe Sugar has a trumpet in the attic," whispered Norma Jean.

"You'll have to ask her," said Bailey. "Now be quiet. You're going to get me in trouble if you don't stop talking."

Norma Jean showed her big, perfect smile.

~ ~ ~

To Bailey's surprise, when Justin got off the bus he said good-bye to Norma Jean.

"See ya later," said Norma Jean, waving happily.

The girls had barely changed into their jeans when Norma Jean looked out the window and said, "There's that boy again."

She hurried outside and called to Justin, who was circling around on his bicycle. He popped a wheelie before screeching to a halt.

Bailey watched from her bedroom as Norma Jean knelt down to pet his brown dog, and talked with him.

Wait 'til I tell Emily, Bailey thought. *Justin is actually speaking to her. Go figure.*

When Norma Jean came back in, she was bubbling with excitement.

"Guess what! Justin collects old bottles that he finds in the woods and he has a crow and he makes things, like a dollhouse for his sister. I asked him if it was okay to come over to his house someday and he didn't say no. I told him I wanted to see Chuck."

"Who's Chuck?" asked Bailey, hardly believing what Norma Jean said.

"Chuck the crow. He had a broken wing when Justin found him, and now he is pretty tame."

Bailey was trying to picture Justin and the crow, when Norma Jean said, "Let's ask Sugar if we can visit his house sometime.

"You ask," said Bailey, not sure she wanted to go there.

21

Cuckoo and Trevilians

"No, I don't have a trumpet," said Sugar as the girls ate red seedless grapes and Swiss cheese cubes for their after-school snack.

Norma Jean looked disappointed.

"But, I do have my husband's boyhood cornet. After Marty and I were married, he joined a community band. Every Christmas morning he played 'Rudolph the Red-Nosed Reindeer' as a signal that Santa had been to our house. That meant the rest of us could come downstairs to open our presents. I couldn't bear to part with the cornet after he died. Later, we'll go to the attic and look for it," said Sugar.

Norma Jean's dark eyes sparkled with joy. "How cool is that," she said.

"But first, get to work on your homework," said Sugar

Norma Jean said, "For my report on my trip I need to write about something that happened a long time ago here, not just what things are like today. Will you help me, Sugar?"

"Sure. Bailey recently finished a report on the history of gold mining near Contrary Creek. You could mention some of that. But this area also played an important part in the Revolutionary War and the Civil War, which Southerners call the War between the States."

"My dad has told me a little bit about both wars. Sometimes we play games with trivia questions about them. He said it was important to know U.S. history even though we live overseas," said Norma Jean. "We're American citizens, you know."

"He's right," said Sugar.

"So what happened here?"

As Bailey half listened while she did her math homework, Sugar asked Norma Jean, "Did you see signs pointing to Cuckoo as you drove into town?"

Norma Jean said yes.

"And have you heard about the ride of Paul Revere?"

Norma Jean nodded again. "He rode his horse to warn the other colonists that the British troops were coming."

"Six years after that ride, Virginia had its own 'Paul Revere,'" said Sugar. "Cuckoo was a tavern. The tavern was a place where travelers stopped to eat and sleep. One day Jack Jouett, a very tall man, was at the tavern. He heard that British dragoons and horsemen, led by Colonel Tarleton, were headed for Charlottesville about forty miles away. Tarleton and his men planned to capture the rebels—members of the Virginia Legislature, including Thomas Jefferson."

"Jefferson was a president," interrupted Bailey.

"That's right, but he wasn't president until much later—starting in 1801. This was June of 1781, when the Revolutionary War had been under way for five years. Anyway, Jack Jouett correctly figured that the British would take the post road. He knew some shortcuts. He galloped on his horse, Sallie, through plantations, fields and woods, and beat the British to Charlottesville."

"A cat and a horse both named Sallie!" said Norma Jean. "Amazing."

"For his bravery Jack Jouett was given two fine pistols and a sword," said Sugar. "He saved Governor Jefferson, Patrick Henry, Daniel Boone and others."

"Can we go to Cuckoo?" asked Norma Jean, as she made some notes on a piece of paper.

"The original tavern is gone, but Cuckoo is the site of a wonderful brick house," said Sugar. "We can see it on one of our adventures."

"What about the Civil War?" asked Norma Jean.

Bailey put her math homework away and said, "I know about that. Sugar is part of a committee trying to save the Trevilians battlefield. And when they have a reenactment of the battle, she said I can be a reenactor."

"What's that?" asked Norma Jean. "Can I be one, too?"

Sugar laughed. "Reenactors are people who learn about the battle, dress in costumes of that period, and reenact the event on its anniversary so that the history won't be forgotten. The actual battle happened June 11 and 12 in 1864. I'm not sure you will be here this year at that time."

"I'll ask Dad if I can stay," said Norma Jean.

Bailey groaned. Sugar gave her a disapproving look. Bailey was getting too many of them since her half sister arrived.

"Maybe we can e-mail him," said Norma Jean. "How do you spell reenactors?" she asked, chewing on her pencil.

Sugar told her, then said, "And while you are writing things down, it was called the battle of T-r-e-v-i-l-i-a-n Station. It involved the Union Army, which was trying to destroy the railroad, and the Confederates, who were trying to stop them. We'll drive past the battlefield site on the west side of Louisa one of these days," said Sugar. "Trevilian Station was the largest all-cavalry battle of the war."

"Cavalry means horses," said Bailey.

"I know that," said Norma Jean.

Sugar said, "Wait a minute, I have some material in my desk that might help you. She returned with papers from the battlefield foundation about one of the reenactments. She moved her glasses up her nose and read: "The cannon roared, the musket volleys thundered and sabers clashed near historic Brackett's farm."

She added, "The actually battle involved about 9,000 Union soldiers, and 5,000 Confederates, with the Southerners winning after the second day of fierce fighting. You can read the rest."

"Great," said Norma Jean. "You're the best, Sugar."

Just then, Shadow and Sallie raced into the kitchen, skidding to avoid Bailey's purple knapsack. Sallie jumped up on Norma Jean's lap. Shadow rubbed against Bailey's leg before padding over to his water bowl. Bailey opened her science book and sighed. Norma Jean was making herself much too much at home.

22

Attic Treasures

"I'm done with my homework. Can we go to the attic now?" asked Norma Jean.

Bailey said, "Five more minutes for me."

"Help me choose something for supper while Bailey finishes up," Sugar said to the younger girl. They looked in the freezer together.

"I like pork chops," said Norma Jean. "My mother fixes them with apples."

"I have homemade applesauce," said Sugar, reaching for a plastic bag, filled with frozen sauce. "We can defrost both in time for dinner."

"Done," said Bailey, carefully closing her book.

"Where's the attic?" asked Norma Jean.

"Upstairs," said Sugar. "Follow me."

Usually Bailey loved going to the attic, with or without her grandmother. Sugar had told her about her great-great aunt Mae, a spy during World War I, and showed her Mae's hat. It would be Bailey's someday. There were other treasures up there in dusty boxes and old trunks—albums, baby clothes, elegant taffeta dresses and letters from the adventurous wild women in the family. Bailey liked to read in the attic on rainy days. It was her special private place, but this was different. Her heart sank at the thought of sharing it with nosy Norma Jean.

Sugar pulled the thin rope that lowered the concealed steps to the hall outside Bailey's bedroom.

"Wow!" said Norma Jean, her dark eyes shining. "I've never seen stairs like this."

"Hang on and watch your step," said Sugar.

"All this stuff is yours?" said Norma Jean in amazement when she reached the top.

"I inherited most of it, but, yes, some is mine that I bought on treasure hunts," said Sugar.

"What's this?" Norma Jean wrapped a yellow feathery scarf around her neck.

"That's my grandmother's boa. She looked elegant when she went dancing in it," said Sugar.

"And this?" Norma Jean said as she picked up everything for a closer look. Each time, Bailey cringed, worrying that Norma Jean would damage something.

"Those were her long kid gloves. They went up her arms above her elbows."

"Look at this," said Norma Jean. She showed them a large gold box.

"That holds my great-grandmother's fan," said Sugar. "She carried it at her wedding."

Norma Jean lifted the lid. Sugar said, "Wait, let me show it to you. It is very fragile."

She gently lifted the fan out of the box and spread it open. Norma Jean carefully studied the blue peacocks, tiny pink flowers and gold inlay in the ivory slats, and the white satin ribbons.

"I've never seen anything so pretty," she said. "May I sketch it sometime?"

Sugar nodded, but reminded Norma Jean that she was not to handle it herself.

Bailey hoped Norma Jean would not notice Mae's red hatbox.

"Where's the cornet?" Norma Jean asked, suddenly remembering their mission.

"Over here," said Sugar as she moved boxes.

She pulled out a brown leather case with black, well-worn handle, then unsnapped the clasp. Inside were a shiny, silver cornet and the monogrammed linen handkerchief that Grampa used to polish it.

"Go ahead, try it," said Sugar.

"It's smaller than my trumpet," said Norma Jean as she inserted the mouthpiece and put it to her lips.

Even Bailey had to admit that she made a nice sound with it.

"I wish I had my music with me," said Norma Jean as she blew a few more notes.

"Mercy," said Sugar, looking at her wrist-watch with the brown leather band. "Time to put it away and go down to get supper started. I'll need help in the kitchen if we are going eat at a decent hour."

The horn went back in its case, and Sugar tucked it among the boxes.

Bailey was relieved that the visit to the attic was brief this time.

23

The Sleepover Begins

Ten girls were invited to the sleepover instead of seven. Norma Jean made friends on her own—girls Bailey didn't know very well—and she asked Sugar if they could come.

Sugar said, "Of course, but leave room for me on the floor." Her face crinkled happily.

When they got home from school on Friday, Sugar was taking laundry out of the dryer.

"You girls can sort what's in the basket and put your own things away. Your company will be here in just two hours. Bailey, please, run the vacuum in the living room. Norma Jean, you can help me arrange the paper cups and plates on the kitchen table," she said.

The doorbell rang promptly at six o'clock. Emily was the first to arrive. She carried her sleeping bag and a shopping bag with her toothbrush, pajamas, and a large stuffed bear. Within what seemed like seconds, more cars pulled up and suddenly the house was noisy and crowded. Norma Jean showed the girls where to put their sleeping bags and jackets and, without asking, offered tours of the house.

"You'll love Bailey's room," she said as all but Emily followed her upstairs.

Bailey pulled her friend aside and took her in Sugar's office to use the computer. She closed the door.

From: "Bailey"<baileyfish@gmail.com>
To: <jbs25@yermail.net>
Sent: 6:27 p.m.
Subject: NSSC rules

Cuttenclip. Emily and I think the first rule is that we will meet every Friday after school. No excuses or you're out. And we'll sign off our e-mail with NSSCR for No Sisters Sisters Club Rocks.

"Quick, back to the party," said Bailey, logging off. "We'll check her answer later."

Bailey turned out the light, closed the office door, and headed to the kitchen.

~ ~ ~

Sugar put the extra-large pizzas, two with just cheese, and one with everything, in the oven to keep warm. She finished the salad and shook a handful of slivered carrots on it.

"I never saw so many books in somebody's house," said Beth as she found Sugar in the kitchen. Bailey and Emily were setting juice and soda bottles on the counter.

"We both like to read," said Sugar, as she mixed the salad dressing with a wooden spoon.

"Is it true that Norma Jean is going to stay longer? She says she wants to be a reenactor."

Sugar sighed. "Norma Jean's plans aren't certain," she told Beth.

"I really like her. Bailey is lucky to have a surprise sister," Beth said to Sugar.

Bailey groaned that so only Emily could hear.

"We were surprised," said Sugar. She dried her mixing bowl and cutting board, and put them away.

"Norma Jean drew us a picture of her—their—father," said Beth. "I think Bailey looks like him."

"I'd like to see those pictures later," said Sugar. "Now, would you let the girls know that I'm taking the pizzas out of the oven? Everybody needs to wash up."

"Sure," said Beth, hurrying out of the room.

24

No-Sleeping Sleepover

"I've never seen such a hungry group," Sugar told the girls. "Did you save room for popcorn?"

That was a silly question. She couldn't make it fast enough. The girls were in their pajamas watching *The Lion King*, and then *Aladdin*, both requested by Norma Jean.

After the videos were done, the girls lined up to use the downstairs bathroom. Sugar read in her office for awhile then checked on everybody one more time before heading for bed.

The girls were getting along, and Bailey and Norma Jean seemed responsible so Sugar decided she would sleep in her own bed. She didn't think things would get out hand. Bailey waved good night to her grandmother. She was glad that she was sleeping between Emily and Beth instead of next to her sister. Norma Jean seemed perfectly happy on the other side of the room as she whispered with her new friends, Clarice, Moneeka, and Brandi.

Just as Bailey dozed, Norma Jean said, "Hey, everyone, I've got a joke. What do you get when you cross a cat with an orange?"

Moneeka said, "A hairy fruit?"

Clarice said, "I give up."

"Meow-malade. I heard that from Peter Williams," said Emily.

"So did I," said Norma Jean. "He's cute."

"He likes Hillary."

"Gumballs," said Norma Jean. "I want him to like me!"

"Shhh," said Bailey. "It's time to sleep."

"Nobody sleeps at a sleepover," said Norma Jean.

"I do," said Bailey.

"I don't," said Shaunda.

"Here's another joke," said Norma Jean. "How can you go for four days without any sleep and not be tired?"

Moneeka guessed, "Sleep at night instead of days?"

"You got it," said Norma Jean.

"Sleeping at night is a good idea," said Bailey.

"Not at a party," said Norma Jean.

Someone giggled. Then someone else made a funny noise that sounded like air escaping from a balloon.

"Pee-you," squealed Norma Jean, starting the laughter—everyone but Bailey joining in.

"See," said Norma Jean, when they stopped laughing. "Nobody sleeps."

"Good night," said Bailey, putting her pillow over her head.

When it was finally quiet, Bailey drifted off to sleep, dreaming of an emerald palace where she was wearing ruby slippers.

BLLAAAAAAHHHH

What on earth was that noise? Bailey wondered as she sat up in confusion. The other girls were also awake and Clarice was crying.

Blaa blaa bla blaa bla blaa bla

Sugar rushed into the room and flicked on the overhead light. There, standing on the arm of the couch, was Norma Jean, dressed in her red silky pajamas, with the yellow feather boa draped around her neck. The mouthpiece of the cornet was pressed to her lips as she tried to play "Rudolph."

"Good grief," said Sugar, comforting Clarice. "Do you know what time it is?"

"Four A.M.," said Norma Jean. "I heard the clock strike before I went up to the attic. I bet

I can play the entire thing without any music."

"Play it," shouted Emily. "I want to hear more." The girls clapped.

"Not tonight, young lady," said Sugar. "But you can give us a concert at breakfast."

Norma Jean made a deep bow, then handed over the cornet. "I just love surprises like this at a sleepover," she said with a big grin that showed every perfect, white tooth.

I don't, thought Bailey as she buried her head under her pillow. *Especially when they involve Norma Jean.*

"Your sister is really funny," whispered Emily.

"Yeah, right," said Bailey.

Emily said, "Are you really going to keep her out of No Sisters Sisters Club? She's really only a half sister, and I like her a lot."

Bailey pretended she was asleep and didn't answer.

25

Guilty Feelings

"That was such a great party," said Norma Jean. "I've never had so much fun in my life."

She tried to hug Bailey, who resisted, then she wrapped her arms around Sugar. "You are the best honorary grandma," she said.

"You're the best honorary granddaughter," replied Sugar. "But now we've got some cleaning up to do."

Norma Jean had a big cheery smile. "I always help my mother clean."

Sugar added, "I've got to say that I enjoyed hearing you play the cornet, not in the middle of the night, but at breakfast. Next time you visit, bring your trumpet and your music, and we'll really have a fine concert."

Was her grandmother encouraging Norma Jean to come back? Bailey didn't get it. Sugar handed each of them a plastic bag to collect the remaining trash from the party.

Bailey found half a slice of cheese pizza under the sofa, and a crust between the seat cushion and arm of her grandmother's favorite chair. Norma Jean picked up cups and napkins, then Bailey ran the vacuum cleaner to suck up spilled popcorn.

As they moved chairs and tables back where they belonged, the phone rang.

They heard Sugar say, "Missing? For how long? Sure, I'll keep an eye out."

Bailey was about to ask Sugar what she was supposed to be watching for when Norma Jean laughed. "Look at Sallie." The kitten's head was stuck in a paper cup. She banged into chairs and tables until the cup fell off.

"Silly baby," said Bailey as she rubbed her silky belly. Sallie purred.

Norma Jean said she wanted to take the first shower, so Bailey turned on the computer to check her e-mail.

There was one from her mother:

From: <Mollyf2@travl.net>
To: "Bailey"<baileyfish@gmail.com>
Sent: 11:02 p.m.
Subject: what's cooking

Dearest Bailey—I've been learning how to cook Costa Rican food. Lots of rice and beans called gallo pinto, which we eat even for breakfast, and delicious coconut flan—it's like a custard. We eat a lot of bananas and papayas. When we put fruit out on the bird feeder near the lodge, it attracts an incredible array of colorful birds—see the attached picture of a toucan. I've met some fascinating fellow travelers, including an American entomologist—that means he studies insects—and we do have lots of bugs here.

How are you and Norma Jean getting along? When does she leave? All my love, Mom

jpg.toucan

Bailey decided to answer her later. There was also one from Amber.

From: <jbs25@yourmail.net>
To: "Bailey"<baileyfish@gmail.com>
Sent: 5:45 p.m.
Subject: guess what

He KISSED ME!!!!!!! Mrs. Mossbagger went to get popcorn during the movie and Ritchie gave me a kiss in the middle of my right cheek. OK, it wasn't a big kiss, but it was a kiss. I couldn't believe it. I told Heather so you can tell Emily.

No Sisters Sisters Club meeting next Friday OK with Heather. NSSCR. Amber

"What's the No Sisters Sisters Club?" asked Norma Jean. Bailey hadn't heard her come into the room. She was reading over Bailey's shoulder. Bailey quickly closed Amber's message.

"Nothing," said Bailey. Her face felt hot.

"I like clubs," said Norma Jean. "At home I've been in Band Club, Art Club, Math Club, Science Club, Dance Club, Government Club and Spanish Club. Can't I be in the Sisters Club? I'm really good at clubs."

She looked genuinely hurt when Bailey mumbled no.

As Bailey shut down the computer, she realized with a sinking feeling that this club wasn't as much fun when the person who was being kept out knew about it.

26

Justin's House

"Justin's mother said it would be okay to visit later this afternoon, so I need to see what I have in the freezer to take along," said Sugar, as she hung up the phone.

"Why do we need to take something?" asked Norma Jean, as she pulled her hair back into a ponytail.

"It's neighborly," said Sugar, opening the freezer door. "Besides, they are having a hard time since Mr. Rudd was arrested."

"Arrested?" Norma Jean's eyes opened wide. "For what?"

Sugar said, "For hurting his kids and polluting Contrary Creek. He hasn't gone to trial yet, but I don't think he is going to bother anybody anytime soon. Now, I've got an extra meatloaf, and some frozen beans from last summer, a peach pie, and a loaf of homemade bread. That ought to do it. Hand me that basket, please."

Bailey helped Sugar pack the food, while Norma Jean continued with her questions. "Is that why Justin seems so sad all the time?"

Bailey wondered where Norma Jean came up with ideas like this. She hadn't thought about how Justin felt—ever. She had only thought about how she felt about her mother leaving, and Norma Jean barging into her life.

Sugar said, "I haven't seen him very much, but it wouldn't surprise me if he is upset, and worried about his mother and little sisters. His father made plenty of money, but didn't take care of his family very well."

Norma Jean thought for a minute then said, "I'm going to get one of my pictures to cheer them up." She hurried up to her room.

Bailey felt uneasy about visiting the Rudd house. She had not met Justin's mother, still wasn't sure about Justin himself, and was a little worried that Fern might be embarrassed to have her reading buddy see her house. Worst of all, Bailey realized that Norma Jean was the one with all the good ideas for doing nice things, and that she, Bailey, had nothing to give. She looked out the kitchen window.

There were three red tulips in Sugar's flowerbed. That gave her an idea.

"Sugar, could we take them some flowers?"

"Wonderful! Here are the scissors. Wrap the stems in wet paper towels to keep them fresh," said Sugar, giving Bailey a hug.

After carefully cutting the tulips, Bailey placed them on top of the food in the basket. Norma Jean quickly appeared with one of her drawings of flowers and birds. She rolled it up and taped it before tucking it next to the tulips.

"Let's go," said Sugar, as she grabbed her keys and purse.

It was a short ride to the dirt road that led to the Rudds' place. Bailey noticed that the gray, two-story house needed painting, but not as much as she had expected. Tricycles and bicycles filled the yard. A honey-colored cat dropped off the porch railing and disappeared as Sugar parked. Bailey thought she could see little faces looking out the window. As she opened the door to the pickup, Justin's brown dog sniffed her knee. She heard Justin whistle and call, "Ninja. Come." The dog turned, then trotted around the side of the house.

Sugar lifted the basket out of the pickup bed, and headed for the porch. At that moment, the door opened and Fern came rushing out, her blond hair streaming behind her.

"Bailey!" she shouted, throwing her arms around her. "Come to my room. We can play a game or something."

"This is my sister, Norma Jean," said Bailey.

Fern said, "You can come, too."

Mrs. Rudd smiled when she saw Sugar and the basket. "You didn't need to," she said.

"My freezer is too full, Nora," said Sugar. "You'll be helping me out."

Bailey knew that wasn't exactly true, but it seemed to make Mrs. Rudd feel better.

"And look at these flowers and oh my, this lovely picture!" Justin's mother said. She pulled two coffee cups out of the cupboard and put the teakettle on the stove. Bailey counted three other little girls, who all had Fern's blue eyes. Two were blond, and one had dark hair like Justin. Fern was dragging her toward the stairs when Justin came in.

"I thought you wanted to see Chuck," he said. He sounded disappointed.

"We do," said Bailey, "but Fern wants me to see her room first."

"I'll go with you," said Norma Jean to Justin.

There was no way Bailey could get out of seeing Fern's room, so she let herself be led upstairs while Norma Jean went outside. The house was neat and clean everywhere Bailey looked.

Fern read three books to her, then showed Bailey her favorite bear she called Fuzzy Marie.

"Will you read with me this summer so I don't forget how?" asked Fern.

"That would be fun," said Bailey. "And you won't forget. You are a good reader now. Let's go see Chuck."

As they passed the kitchen, Bailey could hear Sugar and Mrs. Rudd talking. She saw Justin's mother wipe her eyes with a tissue and Sugar pat her hand. "It will all work out, Nora," Sugar said.

27

Chuck the Crow

"I'll race you," said Fern, as she and Bailey jumped off the bottom porch step. Fern was fast, but Bailey let her win. They found Justin and Norma Jean near a barn. The door was open. Bailey could see an old orange tractor, the black pickup truck that Justin's father used to dump chemicals into Contrary Creek, tires, tools and rusty barrels. There were several junk cars behind the barn, and vines had grown over two of them.

"Look at this," said Norma Jean. A large, shiny, black bird with black eyes was sitting on Justin's arm. Norma Jean held out dried corn in the palm of her hand. Chuck studied her for a moment before accepting the treat.

"I found him when he was just a few weeks old," said Justin. "He fell out of a nest and somehow hurt his wing. He still can't fly very well and I'm not sure he ever will."

"Justin read all about crows on the Internet at school," said Norma Jean, "so he knows just what to feed Chuck, and he's going to let him be wild someday."

"When Chucky was little, we had to feed him stuff like oatmeal and hardboiled eggs," said Fern. "I got to help." Justin rumpled her hair.

"Do you want to feed him?" Fern asked Bailey.

"Sure," said Bailey, even though she wasn't sure. She had never fed a bird before, at least not like that. Chuck stretched out his neck and cocked his head.

"He won't peck you," said Fern. "I feed him all the time."

Bailey stretched out her open hand, and Chuck snapped up the corn kernel. He walked up and down Justin's arm before the boy put him on top of a stack of wooden crates next to the barn door.

"He's really cool," said Bailey.

"Yeah," said Justin.

Norma Jean said, "You should see what Justin makes." She darted into a small shed. "Come on, Bailey. It's really neat. "

The shed was filled with scraps of lumber that Justin had found or had been given at construction sites. With them he made shelves, birdhouses and decorative wooden boxes. His tools were neatly organized on a pegboard and workbench.

"Look at this," said Norma Jean. She held up a box about eight inches long and two inches wide. A crow was carved into the lid.

"It's not done yet," said Justin, looking pleased, "but you can have it for your pencils."

"Awesome," said Norma Jean, beaming. "Thanks."

Caw caw!

"Someone is coming," said Justin. "Chuck always lets me know."

"It's Sugar and Mom," said Fern.

The little girls were following them. Sugar said, "Justin, I hear you are taking good care of the crow. Not everyone takes the time to learn about what they need to eat."

Justin stood up straighter and said, "I really try."

"We've got to get going," said Sugar. "I have several things to do before supper."

"Come back soon," said Mrs. Rudd.

Fern clung to Bailey's hand all the way to the pickup. "I'm glad you came to my house.

You're my friend," said the little girl as Bailey smiled.

After the truck door closed, Norma Jean said happily, "I told you Justin was nice."

"I guess," said Bailey under her breath.

28

Close Call

"Why is Sugar so upset?" asked Norma Jean, as she rocked in Bailey's purple chair.

Bailey leaned back in Sugar's rocker and propped her feet on the porch railing. "I think she had a phone call from the guy who owns the Emmett farm," she said.

"So?" Norma Jean peeled the plastic wrap off a cheese stick.

"So he visited it last weekend and saw even more vandalism, this time inside. Somebody broke in. He is sure someone is deliberately trying to wreck the house so he'll sell it and the land."

"That's awful," said Norma Jean.

"Sugar told him she heard a car screeching away in the night from that direction," said Bailey.

"I've got an idea," said Norma Jean. "Let's go to the farmhouse. I haven't seen it yet."

"Sugar said we can't go without her."

"Sugar said we can't go *in* it without her, not just go and *look* at it," said Norma Jean with a sly grin.

Bailey rocked in silence while she thought. Norma Jean was right, sort of. There might not be any harm in just looking.

"Okay," she said, glancing at her watch. "We have about an hour before Sugar gets back from her historical society meeting."

Norma Jean tucked a small sketch pad and a pencil in her jacket pocket.

Because Bailey and Sugar had walked so many paths in the woods around her grandmother's property, she was familiar with the one that led to the old house. She hurried, making Norma Jean run to keep up. She was afraid that if they walked slowly Norma Jean would want to stop and draw everything, like the yellow flowers along the path, and then they would be late getting home.

Ahead, through a clearing, they could see the Emmett house. Bailey was about to break into a run to the front porch when she heard a car door slam. She stopped so quickly that Norma Jean bumped into her.

"Shhhh," she said.

"Why?" whispered Norma Jean.

"Someone else is here."

"Maybe it's Sugar," said Norma Jean.

"Doubt it," whispered Bailey. "She usually walks."

"Maybe it's that guy, Will."

"Doubt it," whispered Bailey.

"Let's see who it is," said Norma Jean.

"We need to hide," said Bailey. "Let's circle around to the back, but stay behind trees. And be quiet. No talking."

"Do you think I'm crazy?" whispered Norma Jean.

Bailey led the way as they hid behind the tall oaks and hickory trees, ducking low behind bushes until they could see the back of the house. Bailey held her finger to her lips, cautioning Norma Jean to remain silent. A maroon SUV was parked near the back porch where it wasn't visible from the street. The driver's door was open, and a man wearing a black quilted jacket was on the porch trying to pull a piece of plywood off one of the kitchen windows.

"Look, he has a can of spray paint," whispered Bailey. When the man couldn't remove the board, he looked around like he was afraid he was being followed. He aimed the spray paint at the window and wrote: BTH.

"What does that mean?" asked Norma Jean, pulling out her sketchbook.

"I have no idea," said Bailey, secretly glad that her sister was sketching the car, the man and the mysterious letters.

"Can you read the license plate?"

"No, just a J," whispered Norma Jean. "But if I can just get closer . . ." She moved nearer to the edge of the woods. Bailey grabbed her jacket and said, "No you don't." Norma Jean's foot cracked a branch and the man spun around, searching for the source of the sound.

"We'd better go!" said Bailey.

"I haven't finished," said Norma Jean.

"Finish it later. Let's go, and fast."

As soon as they got to the path, the girls ran until they reached the house just as Sugar drove up. They were both out of breath.

"Are you going to tell her? She might get mad," said Norma Jean.

"It was your big fat idea to go," said Bailey. "Of course we have to tell her. She's trying to protect the farm for Will Keswick."

Sugar studied Norma Jean's sketch and listened to their story. Concern filled her face and she wasn't smiling.

"You know you should not have gone without me, even if you weren't planning to go inside. But I'm glad you got this information. I need to call the sheriff and Will, Now, time for homework."

"I'm glad she didn't yell at us," said Norma Jean, opening her school notebook.

"That doesn't mean she isn't upset," said Bailey.

They tried to hear what Sugar was saying on the phone in the other room, but her voice was too soft.

When Sugar came back into the kitchen she said, "The sheriff wants to see your sketch. He doesn't know what BHT means, but he plans to send extra patrols to the area."

Sugar rinsed the lettuce for salad and said firmly, "Be observant, but don't go back to the Emmett house again. It's too dangerous."

"Okay," said Norma Jean.

Bailey said, "We won't!" She meant it.

29

Sallie Slips Out

In the time since Norma Jean had arrived, more flowers—especially red, yellow, and orange tulips—were blooming around Sugar's front porch. Bailey was amazed at how quickly the leaves appeared on the trees.

Her grandmother said that later in the summer they would see sunflowers, taller than the girls, growing where seeds had taken root under the wild bird feeder.

Sugar showed the girls where tiny apples were developing after the blossoms had blown off the trees, and where chipmunks lived in the woodpile.

Bailey pointed at a downy woodpecker in the hollow of a maple tree. Sugar said it was looking for grubs and insects. Bluebirds were making a nest in a birdhouse in the front yard.

"I like all the seasons," continued Sugar, "but spring is my favorite. There are so many beautiful flowers. The hummingbirds will be back soon. And maybe purple martins will move into their 'apartment house.'"

"Purple martins?" asked Norma Jean.

Sugar pointed to a large white birdhouse with many holes in it. "That's for the martins. They eat mosquitos, which is why we want to attract them."

She pushed her hair away from her forehead. "But I also like summer, especially when the lightning bugs make it look like fireworks in the woods. And when the tree frogs call to each other. I like to sit on the porch on summer evenings and listen to the sounds of the night."

"What about fall?" asked Bailey.

Sugar said, "We wild women like fall. The bright colors in the trees make us want to roam one last time before winter. We pick apples and freeze or can fruit and vegetables to enjoy during the winter months."

"What about winter?" asked Norma Jean.

"Winter is beautiful here, even though it is cold some days," said Sugar. "You can't image how nice a dull brown yard looks when it is covered with a dusting of white," she said with a smile. "I like to look for animal tracks in the snow—fox, rabbit and deer. And I watch nuthatches, chickadees, and finches at the feeder. Now, I have some work to do. What are your plans?"

"Let's go to the cemetery one more time before Dad comes back," said Norma Jean. "I really like walking in the woods."

"Okay," said Bailey. It was going with Norma Jean, or staying home by herself.

"Help yourself to some snacks to take along," said Sugar. "You can work up quite an appetite on a walk."

As the back door closed behind Norma Jean, Sallie slipped through.

"Put her back inside," said Bailey.

"She'll be fine," said Norma Jean. "Sallie just wants to have an adventure, too."

"She should stay here," said Bailey.

"Oh, okay," said Norma Jean, as she picked up Sallie and put her inside. But Norma Jean was in a hurry and didn't notice that the screen door didn't close all the way.

It didn't take Sallie long to push it open and bound down the steps after the girls.

30

Cat-snatcher

Bailey dropped her backpack containing two bananas and two bottles of water against a large fallen tree and pulled her Oz book out of the zippered pocket. The earth, covered with leaves, was still cool. Green ferns and ground pine pushed through here and there. She found a patch of sunlight to sit in, spread a small blue-plaid blanket next to the tree, and opened her book.

Norma Jean straddled the far end of a long log, placing her notebook and pencils on it in front of her. She faced the tombstones so she could sketch them.

Meow!

Both girls whirled around.

"What's Sallie doing here?" asked Bailey, crossly. "I told you to put her in the house."

"I *did*," said Norma Jean. "I don't know how she got out. Here, Sallie. Good girl."

"Well, keep an eye on her," said Bailey, as she watched Sallie stalk a rust-colored butterfly with brown spots that managed to stay just out of reach of her paws.

Bailey turned to page 242 of the *Emerald City of Oz*. She read about the Flutterbudgets—people who were worried about all the "what-ifs." Bailey knew she was one of them. She was always worried. What if something happened to her mother while she was traveling, or to Sugar, or to her wonderful kittens?

Bailey was nearing the end of the book and hadn't made up her mind which of the Oz series to read next. It was a toss-up between *The Patchwork Girl of Oz* and *Rinkitink in Oz*—she liked the covers of both. And even though the books were sometimes silly, they often contained new ideas to think about, such as Flutterbudgets.

After reading for fifteen minutes, Bailey stretched and reached for a bottle of water.

"Want some?" she asked Norma Jean, who didn't answer. She was busy drawing.

Bailey walked over to see how her sketches were coming.

Norma Jean had started by drawing the tall cedars that framed the little family cemetery. While Bailey watched, she penciled in Sallie leaping for the butterfly.

"I don't know how you do that," said Bailey, wishing she was that artistic.

"I just do it," said Norma Jean, not looking up. "Anyone can draw. It just takes practice."

As Bailey returned to her spot, moving her blanket slightly to stay in the sun, Sallie crept up on the large mossy, brown tombstone.

Bailey smiled as she watched the kitten pounce on an imaginary mouse in the leaves.

Then, Sallie peeked around the tombstone, her black tail with the white tip twitching as she slipped behind it.

"Gotcha," said a voice that sounded like a branch scraping on the side of a house.

Bailey and Norma Jean looked at each other in confusion.

"Where have you been, Bootsie? I've been looking everywhere for you."

The girls jumped to their feet and rushed to the gravestone.

An old woman, with hair that looked like she had stuck her finger in an electrical socket, was sitting under a bush. She wore a lumpy green coat, fuzzy pink slippers and an ankle-length, yellow-flowered flannel nightgown. Her fierce blue eyes stared at the girls like she could see through them. She clutched Sallie.

"That's my kitten," said Bailey.

"My cat," said the old woman. Sallie squirmed in her arms, but the woman was not about to let go.

Meow, cried Sallie.

"Please let me have her," said Bailey.

"Mine," said the old woman.

"Please let her go," pleaded Bailey.

"My cat," said the woman.

Norma Jean and Bailey exchanged worried looks.

"I'll give you a banana," said Norma Jean, "if you give us the kitten."

The woman seemed to consider it, but then said, "Bootsie doesn't like bananas. Go away."

"What are we going to do?" Bailey whispered to Norma Jean. "I told you not to bring Sallie."

"I didn't bring her. She just got out," said Norma Jean. She looked scared. "I don't know what to do."

"Think of something," said Bailey, ready to cry.

The old woman rummaged around under the branches, and pulled out a pillowcase. She seemed to have forgotten about the girls, who were watching her closely.

Norma Jean thought for a minute and then whispered, "I've got an idea."

She ran back to where she had dropped her papers and quickly sketched the old woman's face and wild hair. It wasn't very detailed, but it looked like the cat-snatcher.

"What's that for?" asked Bailey.

"I'll be right back. I'll go get Sugar. She might know who she is. You stay here to make sure that woman doesn't leave with Sallie."

"Okay, but hurry! Hurry!" whispered Bailey. "Run!"

"I'll run like Jack Jouett," said Norma Jean as she shoved the sketch in her pocket and dashed off through the woods, dodging branches and jumping over logs.

In her high scratchy voice the woman sang, "I love little kitty her coat is so warm . . . ." She was petting the squirming kitten.

I hope she doesn't hurt Sallie, worried Bailey. She was glad that Norma Jean was racing for help, but wished someone was with her in the woods right now. She had felt safer when her sister was there.

"We're going home, Bootsie," the old woman said. "Warm milk and catnip for you."

The old woman stood up. Bailey could not see her kitten. Then she realized that the woman had put Sallie in the pillowcase. Sallie was mewing in terror and thrashing around.

"Please let me have my kitten. Her name is Sallie, not Bootsie," begged Bailey.

"Mine," said the old woman as she shuffled away into the woods.

31

Rescued

Bailey knew she had to follow the woman and Sallie, but how would Norma Jean and Sugar know where to find them? What could she use to point the way? Then she remembered that Norma Jean said it didn't matter what you used as a pointer as long as it was obvious. The two bananas! She reached into her backpack, broke one banana in half, and fashioned an arrow by using both halves and the one whole one between them.

Bailey pointed the arrow in the direction that the old woman had headed. She followed a few paces behind, hoping that the woman would drop the sack. Then she had another thought. Maybe she could snatch the sack out of the old woman's hands and run for home with it.

The mewing was even more pitiful.

"I'm coming, Sallie," Bailey whispered. "I'll rescue you."

She tried to walk silently so that the woman wouldn't hear her creeping up from behind, but she tripped over a branch and it snapped.

The old woman turned around and peered, but she didn't see Bailey hiding behind the trunk of a large oak tree.

When she was satisfied that she was alone, the old women continued walking. Her pace quickened.

That was close, thought Bailey. As she followed the old woman, Bailey made another arrow pointer, this time with five rocks that she found, and another with three sticks.

The woman sang, "Humpty-Dumpty sat on a wall. ABCDEDF, tip me over pour me out." She stopped for a rest. Bailey wondered if she could get close enough to grab the pillowcase. She was almost within reach when the woman turned around, nearly bumping into her.

"Go away, Lucille. You can't have her."

"I'm not Lucille. I'm Bailey. Please give me Sallie."

"You can't fool me," said the woman, turning to walk away. She twisted the sack in front of her so that Bailey could not reach it. All Bailey could do was continue to follow quietly, hoping that help would come soon.

They went deeper and deeper into the woods. Bailey made another arrow, this time out of six pine cones.

Where is Norma Jean? worried Bailey. *I hope she didn't get lost. I need help!*

Suddenly Bailey heard rushing steps in the leaves and an unfamiliar voice.

"Miss Dolly," said a woman from the right of them. "I'll bet you are cold and hungry. I have a warm blanket to wrap you in. And I have something special for you."

Bailey turned and saw someone who looked like a nurse. Sugar and Norma Jean were hurrying way behind her.

"I have Pink Baby for you," said the nurse, holding out a small cloth pink doll with yellow yarn hair.

Miss Dolly stopped walking. "Do I know you?" she asked.

"I'm Karen," said the nurse. "I live with you. I'll trade you Pink Baby for what you have in the sack.

"Nothing in the sack," said Miss Dolly.

"Then you won't mind putting it down," said Nurse Karen.

The woman considered the trade while still clutching the squirming pillowcase.

There was a long silence. Bailey held her breath.

"Okay, for Pink Baby and cookies," said Miss Dolly, as she dropped the sack. Out bounded Sallie. She streaked through the woods towards Sugar's house, with Norma Jean and Bailey racing after her.

32

Safe at Last

When they reached Sugar's house, the girls called and called, but they couldn't find the frightened kitten. Sallie wasn't waiting on the porch, like they had expected. Shadow followed them everywhere as they hunted for his sister. Finally, he ducked under the back porch. Bailey and Norma Jean looked into the darkness of the far corner and saw two pairs of eyes.

"It's okay, Sallie," said Bailey. "It's okay, Shadow. She's safe now."

"Come out, Sallie, and we'll rub your belly and give you treats," said Norma Jean. "Good kitty."

The girls finally coaxed the kitten to safety. They were in the kitchen feeding Sallie milk when Sugar and Nurse Karen helped Miss Dolly walk up the back steps.

"You're not bringing *her* in the house?" said Bailey in alarm. She was afraid the old woman would try to capture one of her kittens again and they might not be as lucky this time.

"Don't worry," said Sugar. "She's not going to hurt you or steal Sallie. This is the woman everyone's been looking for. She wandered away from her house and has been sleeping in the woods for a couple of nights."

"She scares me," said Bailey. "She took Sallie, and she didn't believe us."

"I understand," said Sugar, hugging her granddaughter. "She was reliving her childhood and thought Sallie was her own cat."

"She called me Lucille."

"That was her older sister's name," said Sugar.

Bailey and Norma Jean exchanged glances. "The grave with the name 'Lucille,'" whispered Bailey.

"We are glad that you girls found Miss Dolly and that you both had such great ideas to help us identify her and locate you," said Nurse Karen. "We just want to calm her down, and give her something to eat before we take her home."

Sugar looked at Norma Jean. "Your sketch of the woman told us for sure who she was, and Bailey's banana arrow pointed us in the right direction, and then we were able to follow the other pointers. Good thinking." She gave each of them a pat on the back.

Bailey looked in the living room. She saw that the nurse had brushed the wildness out of Miss Dolly's hair and was wiping the old woman's hands and face with a warm cloth. Miss Dolly's eyes were closing. She looked fragile, papery, and not at all dangerous when she was wrapped in a green fuzzy blanket.

Sugar said, "Karen, I'll give you a hand getting her home. I think we need to call the sheriff to let him know that she's been found alive and okay. I know everyone has been worried."

Nurse Karen said, "Thanks so much, folks, for helping us. If you don't mind, Norma Jean, I'd like to keep that sketch of her. It is very good."

Norma Jean beamed. "I'll make you a new one, now that her hair is fixed up nicely," she said. She placed Pink Baby in Miss Dolly's lap.

"That would be wonderful," said the nurse. "I'm sure her daughter and grandson will appreciate that. Miss Dolly was once a fine artist. She painted in oils. And she could sing with the most beautiful voice and she taught piano. Everyone loved Miss Dolly."

Both girls looked at her in astonishment.

When Sugar saw their faces she said, "I guess I should explain. Miss Dolly was Mr. Emmett's younger cousin. He adored her. Even though she was married, everyone still calls her Miss Dolly, just as he always did."

"Then she was the one who played his piano in the old house?" said Bailey.

"That's right," said Sugar. "She was very sad when Lucille died when they were children, and so she always left toys by her grave. Some little dishes are still there."

"I get it," said Norma Jean, smiling at Bailey.

"Miss Dolly has her good days, but more and more she lives in the past," said Nurse Karen. "It would be nice if you would come to visit sometime on a good day. I'll show you her paintings."

"Really? I'll draw her a picture of Bootsie," said Norma Jean.

"Maybe we can bake cookies for her," said Bailey, still trying to imagine a younger Miss Dolly singing and painting fine pictures.

"Let's go," said Sugar. "You girls get cleaned up while I help get Miss Dolly back to her house, and then we will have the supper of suppers and you can help me fix it."

"What will it be?" asked Norma Jean.

"I have no idea," said Sugar, "but it will be a refrigerator adventure."

Later, as the girls stretched out with the kittens on Bailey's bed, Norma Jean said, "I'm really sorry about Sallie getting out. And I'm sorry I make you mad. I wish we could be friends."

Bailey looked at Norma Jean's face. She seemed genuinely sad.

"I didn't mean to be so mean," said Bailey. She stroked Shadow as he stretched one silky paw. "I'm sorry, too. I was really proud of how you helped save Sallie."

"I wish I could stay longer," said Norma Jean, rubbing Sallie behind the ears.

Bailey didn't answer right away. Then, she smiled like she did when she saw her best friends, and made the sign for sister.

"Sisters," said Norma Jean, happily

33

More E-mail

When Bailey logged on the computer, she found another cheery e-mail from her mother, with again no mention of coming back for a visit or to live. Instead, Mom seemed to be getting increasingly interested in what she was seeing and learning in Costa Rica, and especially bugs.

From: <Mollyf2@travl.net>
To: "Bailey"<baileyfish@gmail.com>
Sent: Sunday, 2:06 p.m.
Subject: leafcutters

Bailey dearest: Andrew and I–he's the entomologist–went deep into the rain forest yesterday with our guide Jose. Andrew wanted to show me the leafcutter ants. They can remove all the leaves from a mango tree in just one night. They march in a line through the jungle carrying huge pieces of leaves on their backs. And we saw the most amazing collection of butterflies early one morning. Our guide spoke to each one as if it were a special friend. Some sat on his finger. I had never realized how interesting bugs and insects could be. There is so much to learn here. Our guide also showed us a yellow viper, a small but very deadly snake. But don't worry, I'm in good hands. I will probably write an article about Andrew at some point. Another box of presents, including molas from Panama, is headed your way. Write me, love and kisses, Mom

Bailey couldn't believe it. Mom likes bugs? This was crazy. When they lived in Florida her mother became upset if she saw giant palmetto bugs in the kitchen or spiders as big as her hand on the walls. She made Bailey catch lizards and put them outside, and jumped if she saw a snake, even a good one, in the garden. Was this what happened when a wild women was off on an adventure?

She e-mailed:

From: "Bailey"<baileyfish@gmail.com>
To: <Mollyf2@travl.net>
Sent: 6:02 p.m.
Subject: bugs

Mom, you're funny. I didn't know you liked bugs. Now you can catch the lizards and put them outside yourself. Hahahha. Norma Jean is leaving soon. She's getting nicer and she helped rescue Sallie when an old lady grabbed her. Miss Dolly was lost and didn't know what she was doing.

We went to her house later and saw her art. She was OK by then. She held my hand and said I had nice fingers for playing the piano. Sugar said if I wanted to learn, she would find a piano and a teacher. Sugar said she always wanted to play. Miss Dolly said Sugar's fingers were pretty short, but if she worked hard she might be able to learn anyway. I've decided to let my hair grow longer, like Norma Jean's. Love, Bailey

And there was one from Amber:

From: <jbs25@yermail.net>
To: "Bailey"<baileyfish@gmail.com>
Sent: 5:42 p.m.
Subject: Forget him

Hey Bailey—It's over. Mrs. Mossbagger heard him tell his doofus friend about the kiss and she called Mom and now we can't get-together anymore. Ritchie said he was sorry, but I saw him talking with April and she told Heather he likes her. Boys! It's really hot here. Mom says we can go to the beach later. Have you thought of any rules yet? NSSCR Amber

Bailey replied:

From: "Bailey"<baileyfish@gmail.com>
To: <jbs25@yermail.net>
Sent: 6:35 p.m.
Subject: sisters club

Too bad about Ritchie. At least you got a kiss. I haven't met anybody yet that I want to kiss. Don't know about rules. Norma Jean isn't so bad after all. Maybe half sisters can join the club. What do you think? NSSCR Bailey

Norma Jean tapped her on the shoulder. "Sugar said I could use her e-mail to write to Dad. Let me know when you are done."

Bailey told her that she was finished and would show her how to use Sugar's computer.

From: "Sugar"<sugarww@earthsave.net>
To: <pjfish2005@yermail.net>
Sent: Sunday 1:45 p.m.
Subject: want to stay

Dad, you will never believe what has been happening. We saved Bailey's cat and are helping Sugar protect an historic house. Can I stay longer? This is so much fun. I just love everybody here. Love, NJ

She asked if Bailey wanted to add a P.S., but Bailey shook her head no. There were things she would like to say to her father, like how Norma Jean was a good artist, but he already knew that. Besides, he hadn't written to just her.

Norma Jean hit the send button as the phone rang. It was Emily.

"Sure," said Bailey, handing the phone to Norma Jean. "She wants to come by on Saturday to say good-bye before you leave."

34

Sirens in the Night

Bailey was dreaming that she was back in Florida watching the end of a parade. The police and firefighters were sounding their sirens as they went by. The noise was so loud that she covered her ears.

"Wake up! Wake up!" shouted Norma Jean, yanking the pillow off Bailey's head. "Don't you hear the sirens? Something big is going on!"

Bailey nearly knocked heads with Norma Jean as she sat up.

"What's happening?"

"I'm not sure, but Sugar told me to wake you up and that we were to stay in the house. She went to the fire."

"What's on fire?"

"She thinks it is the Emmett house. She heard a car screech again and she ran outside in her pajamas to see if she could get a description. She smelled smoke and called 911." Norma Jean was breathless.

Bailey hurried to the window.

There was an orange glow in the distance.

"I hope they get there in time," she said. "I know that Will Keswick really wants to fix up the house."

Bailey shivered, then realized that Norma Jean had grabbed blankets off her bed for both of them.

"Here," said Norma Jean, as she wrapped herself in one.

"I hope Sugar's okay," said Bailey.

"Me, too," said Norma Jean.

Every once in a while they could see flames riding up a pine tree and shooting in the sky.

Then the orange glow dimmed and it was harder to see.

"Let's go downstairs to wait for Sugar," suggested Norma Jean. "We could make nice cocoa."

They had finished the hot chocolate and were dozing next to each other on the couch when Sugar closed the front door.

Her heavy red-plaid jacket smelled like a campfire. She tried to tiptoe past the girls, but Bailey heard her.

"The house has some damage," said Sugar, "but they caught the guy who started the fire. Your description of the SUV matched the one I saw racing down the road. The deputies nabbed him after a few miles. The driver had matches and an empty gasoline can."

"Why did he do it?" said Bailey, wide awake.

"We are pretty sure he was working for the developer who wants the property. He admitted that BTH meant Burn This House. They wrote it on the wall to make sure that whoever was hired to set the fire knew exactly which one it was."

"Can the house be fixed?"

"We can tell more in daylight," said Sugar. "I hope so, but it has some char. Do you want to stay here on the couch, or go back up to bed?"

"I'll stay here with Norma Jean. She'll be worried if she wakes up all alone," said Bailey.

"I'll get your pillows," said Sugar, blowing her a kiss.

35

Meeting Will Keswick

Bailey, Norma Jean, and Emily were moving back and forth on the porch swing when a white pickup truck drove up Sugar's gravel driveway. Its sides and tires were splattered with reddish mud.

"Is your grandmother home?" asked the driver. He was tall and slender, with green eyes, and curly hair the color of a yellow cat. It stuck out under his baseball cap.

"Hey, Will. C'mon in and tell me how things are going," said Sugar. "What can I offer you? Ice water? Coffee?"

Will Keswick wiped his feet on the mat, took off his cap, and stepped inside. The girls followed him, curious to hear about the Emmett house and the fire.

"He's a hunk," whispered Norma Jean.

"Yeah," said Emily tugging her hair.

"Well," he said, taking a seat at the kitchen table while Sugar warmed up the leftover coffee from breakfast, "I think we are going to be able to save it. I'm so grateful that you heard the SUV, Sugar, and that you girls had such useful information."

Sugar said, "Is there much damage?"

"Not as much as we feared. The arsonist started by trying to burn down the old barn, which doesn't have much historical significance. It was flames from the barn that you, and others, saw in the sky. By the time he tried to set a fire at the house, the sheriff and fire department were on the way. So there was damage to the back porch, but I was going to replace it anyway." He smiled broadly.

Sugar said, "I'm so glad. You'll have to evict your upstairs tenants, you know."

"The vultures?" Mr. Will chuckled. "As soon they as are fledged," he said to the girls, "I intend to replace the upstairs windows. The birds will need to find a new place to nest next year, because by then we hope to be in the house at least part time."

"Vultures? You didn't tell me about vultures," said Norma Jean. "I want to draw them."

"With Will's permission, we'll go back after the fire investigation is finished," said Sugar.

"Be sure to take your sketch pad," he said. "Those babies are pretty ugly . . . but I like them anyway."

"What about the piano?" asked Bailey.

"It had smoke and water damage, but I think it can be repaired and restored," said Mr. Will. "My grandmother—you met her—Miss Dolly, gave me lessons when I was a child. I also plan on hanging some of her oil paintings in the house when we are done with the restoration."

"It will be beautiful," said Sugar. "Let us know if we can help with anything. Bailey and I are quite the decorators."

"We fixed up my bedroom and my new porch rocker," said Bailey. "I helped paint."

"We need all the help we can get. My wife and I will have a party for all the neighbors when we are done."

Norma Jean said, "Wait until I come back. I want to go to the party."

Mr. Will said, "That sounds like a good plan. Besides, I'd like you all to meet my boys, Noah and Fred. They are about your age."

Norma Jean grinned. Bailey no longer found that smile annoying.

36

Ice Cream with a Twist

While Sugar was running errands in town, Paul Fish returned earlier than expected.

"Where's your grandmother?" he asked. "I don't see her truck."

Bailey was sitting in her rocker reading the first few pages of *Rinkitink in Oz*. She said, "She'll be back soon. Are you looking for Norma Jean?"

Paul Fish said, "Actually for both of you. It looks like a great day for ice cream. How about the three of us go get some before Norma Jean and I head for airport?"

Bailey said, "I don't know if Sugar would say it's okay. . . ."

Paul Fish smiled warmly and said, "I'm sure it won't be a problem. After all, I *am* your dad and it will be a long time before we get back this way. We'll leave a note for her. She'll understand."

"I don't know," said Bailey. She was uneasy about going anywhere with him without Sugar, but the day was warm and having ice cream sounded good.

"Go find your sister," said Paul Fish, "And be thinking about what kind of ice cream you want. Maybe a banana split," he said with a friendly smile.

I wonder if I should? I guess it's okay. Norma Jean's stuff is still here. Bailey opened the screened door and called upstairs to her sister, who was packing.

"He's here. We're going for ice cream before you leave," said Bailey.

"Hooray!" said Norma Jean. "I'll be down in one minute."

Bailey found a piece of yellow lined paper and wrote a note to Sugar.

Dear Sugar: Our father came back early. I hope you don't mind. We are going with him for ice cream and will be back soon—in time for you to say good-bye to Norma Jean.

Love, Bailey.

She placed the note next to the telephone where Sugar would see it when she returned.

Shadow was by her feet, weaving in and out of her ankles. Bailey stopped to pet him before she took her dark-green windbreaker out of the hall closet. When she opened the front door she thought she saw Paul Fish putting Norma Jean's pink suitcase in the trunk.

That can't be right, she thought. *I thought she was still packing.*

Norma Jean was in the back seat. "This is so much fun," she said.

Bailey still wasn't sure she was making the right decision, but figured they might even be back home before Sugar returned. Then she would say good-bye and have the house to herself again. She would miss Norma Jean more than she ever could have imagined when they first met. She hadn't admitted it at the time, but Norma Jean made her laugh inside on several occasions, like when she played the cornet at the slumber party and woke up everyone. But Bailey was also looking forward to having Sugar to herself, and having Sallie sleep with her.

She closed the car door and Paul Fish started down the driveway.

The ride to town no longer looked unfamiliar as it had just a few months earlier. Bailey liked seeing the Blue Ridge mountains in the distance. They weren't always visible, but today was clear, with sunlight dappling the spring foliage.

Paul Fish was good to his word. The girls were allowed to select their favorite ice cream. Bailey ordered one scoop of chocolate and a second of mint chocolate chip and double the hot fudge. Norma Jean wanted a strawberry and vanilla sundae topped with whipped cream and sprinkles. Their father asked for double scoops of pistachio on a waffle cone, which he said was the biggest he had ever seen.

Bailey was ashamed that she had been concerned about going for the ride. As they ate, Paul Fish asked her questions about school, and the clarinet, and made both of them laugh when he told them he had been a real nerd until he was a junior in high school. He said, "Then I looked in the mirror one day and saw I had become quite a handsome fellow."

He leaned forward confidentially and said, "My friends and I loved to play pranks, especially in Mrs. Brown's class."

"Like what?" asked Norma Jean.

His hazel eyes twinkled and he rubbed his beard. "Almost every day we'd knock under our desks." He demonstrated, making the ice cream clerk turn around. "Mrs. Brown would stop writing on the board and go to the door to see who was there. We fooled her every time."

"Did you ever get in trouble for it?" asked Bailey.

"Never," said Paul Fish. "Remember, I was quite a handsome fellow." His eyes squinted like Bailey's when he smiled.

"You must have been hungry," he said, noticing that the girls were quickly finishing.

"That was good, thank you," said Bailey, as she licked the last of the sticky chocolate off her fingers.

"Yum," said Norma Jean.

"I'm glad you liked it," said Paul Fish. "This is great—seeing both my girls having fun together. I have dreamed of this day for a long time."

They got in the car for the ride back to Sugar's. But soon something was very wrong.

"Where are we going?" asked Bailey as they drove past the turn, the road that they should have taken to Lake Anna.

"I've decided take a different way home," said Paul Fish. "It is such a beautiful day."

"I think we need to go right back," said Bailey, her voice trembling. "The regular way."

"It's a nice day for a little ride," said her father.

Bailey felt increasingly panicked as the miles went by. This wasn't right. Norma Jean seemed totally unconcerned. She was humming "Rudolph."

"Please," said Bailey. "You promised."

"Don't worry," said Paul Fish, "there is another turn somewhere up here. There are many roads that lead to home."

The countryside looked less and less familiar. Bailey knew that she hadn't fully explored the area around Lake Anna, but now she did not recognize any buildings or roads.

What if she was being kidnapped and taken to Guam or wherever her father and his family lived? What if she never saw her mother or Sugar again? Why didn't he take the way home that she knew? She wanted her mother. She wanted Sugar. She wanted Sallie and Shadow, and if she ever got home again she would never leave, not even for a minute. She would be nicer to everyone and help more around the house.

She heard Paul Fish's cell phone ringing. He didn't reach for it right away. The ringing stopped.

Why doesn't he answer it? worried Bailey.

Then it rang again. This time he put it to his ear after the fourth ring.

"Yeah," he said. "Hey, Sugar. Sure, they are with me. We went for ice cream. No need to call the sheriff. Well, I'm not exactly sure where we are. I took a wrong turn." He was silent for a moment.

"Yeah, we're on Payne Mill Road. What's the best way to locate you from here?"

He listened to Sugar's directions.

"Okay, we'll be there soon."

Bailey had never felt more relieved.

When they reached her grandmother's house, Sugar was waiting on the front porch. Bailey opened the door as soon as the car stopped and ran up the steps into Sugar's arms.

Paul Fish and Norma Jean followed.

"Sorry, I didn't mean to worry you," he said, rubbing his beard.

Neither Bailey nor Sugar said anything as they held tight to each other.

"Well, I guess we'd better be going. Little one, check to see that you haven't left anything behind."

Norma Jean went upstairs to look around her room one more time. When she came down Sallie was right behind her.

Norma Jean held two drawings. "I made these for you," she said.

She handed one to Sugar. It was a pencil sketch of Sugar's house, with Sugar standing in the doorway and Bailey sitting on the front steps with Shadow and Sallie.

Sugar said, "Norma Jean, this is beautiful. We'll have to get it framed. I want you to sign it."

Norma Jean handed the second one to Bailey. As Bailey unrolled it, she saw that Norma Jean had sketched a picture of the two of them in the cemetery. It showed Norma Jean drawing a picture while Bailey was reading.

"That was a nice day, wasn't it?" said Norma Jean.

"Yeah. This picture is really great, thanks. I'll hang it next to the wild women," said Bailey. "But I don't have anything to give you."

"That's okay," said Norma Jean. "I have a sister now. That's what counts." She made the sister sign and Bailey did the same.

Norma Jean gave Bailey a big hug, and Bailey willingly hugged back.

"E-mail me?"

"Sure," said Bailey.

"Time to go, kiddo," said Paul Fish. "We have a long trip ahead. Thanks again for everything, Sugar . . . and Bailey."

"I'll come back," said Norma Jean.

"We're changing the name of the club," said Bailey. "It's going to be Best Friends and Sisters Club. You can be in it." Norma Jean smiled her big smile.

"Have a safe trip," Sugar said. "And, hello to Flora and the boys."

Paul Fish turned to Bailey with both hands reaching out. Bailey knew he wanted a hug. Suddenly, she wanted one, too, but she wasn't sure what to do. Everyone was watching.

"Bye," she said, holding out one hand.

"I'm really glad to know you, Bailey. Now, don't forget this handsome fellow," Paul Fish said with a wink. "Next time we'll noodle around on the clarinet and maybe have some just-us time—just Bailey and Dad."

Bailey smiled. She hoped no one could see the lump in her throat.

As the car with Norma Jean waving wildly reached the end of the drive, Sugar said, "C'mon inside." She wrapped her arms around Bailey and mussed her hair.

"Tomorrow we'll have an adventure. We'll look in the attic for frames for our pictures when we pack away Norma Jean's cot."

Bailey thought for a moment, then said, "Maybe we could find a comfortable real bed for her room for when she visits again."

"That's what the wild women would do," said Sugar. Her face crinkled, and she closed the front door behind them.

37

Out of the Drawer

The kittens were waiting on Bailey's bed when she turned down the quilt and blankets. She petted them for a few minutes. It was good to have Sallie back on her pillow again instead of sleeping with Norma Jean.

Bailey thought about reading, but instead of sliding under her covers and opening her book, she walked over to her desk. She pulled open the bottom drawer, lifted out the photo album, and carried it back to her bed. She could hear the grandfather clock bonging nine times in the front hall at the bottom of the stairs, as she sat cross-legged on her patchwork quilt.

Bailey opened the album carefully. She studied the pictures of her parents' wedding, her baby pictures, and finally the one of her father holding her tightly, with that happy and sad expression. She touched his face with her fingers. Bailey thought about the pictures, observing every little detail in them, until the clock struck the half hour. Her face relaxed, and she smiled. *I have a dad.*

Then she put the silver album on the table next to her bed, where she could look at it again in the morning. Every morning.

Book Club Questions

1. Authors try to "show," not "tell" what a character is like. What are some of the things Norma Jean *does* when she first visits Bailey's bedroom that tell us about her personality? What is Bailey's first impression of this half sister and why does she have this reaction?

2. What hints are in the early chapters about what will happen to the Emmett house?

3. Have you ever been in a secret club? Or left out of one? How did you feel about it?

4. Authors try to make characters more believable by presenting their good and bad sides. Norma Jean irritates Bailey in many ways: hugging her in public, answering all the questions in class, touching and then bending Molly's picture from the refrigerator, picking up the toys in the graveyard. But Norma Jean

is not all bad. Give examples of thoughtful or kind things that she does.

5. Many things that Norma Jean does could have more than one interpretation. Are we getting to know Norma Jean solely from Bailey's point of view, or do we also see her a little from Sugar's point of view? Give examples.

6. Try rewriting the scene when Norma Jean first meets Bailey, but tell it in Norma Jean's words.

7. Do you think Norma Jean realizes that Bailey does not like her, or is she not aware of that? Give examples to show Norma Jean knows she does or doesn't feel welcome.

8. Write an e-mail Norma Jean might send to her mother about her visit with Bailey. Have her give her version of the sleepover or her version of the visit to the Emmett house when they saw the man spraypaint the letters BTH, or her version of meeting Miss Dolly in the woods.

9. On p. 146 there is a turning point in the way the two half sisters feel about each other. What happens? Why do you think there is a shift or change?

10. First impressions are not always accurate ones. Tell how this pertains to Miss Dolly.

11. Norma Jean and Paul Fish live very far away from Virginia. Do you think Bailey will ever see them again. Do you think she will ever go to Guam to visit? Do you think she wants to get to know her father, her stepmother and the rest of his family?

12. How do you think Bailey pictured her dad during the years she did not know him? Did she think of him often or not much? Why do you think Sugar welcomed Bailey's questions about her father when her mother did not?

13. When he comes to Sugar's house, Paul Fish has not seen Bailey for almost eleven years. Do you think he tried to contact her earlier? Write a phone conversation between Paul and Molly when he makes an attempt to see Bailey when she is four.

14. Describe how Bailey feels in the car when her dad seems to be lost on the way back to Sugar's house. Why do you think she feels that way? Would you have felt that way, too?

Web Sites

Crows

www.ascaronline.org/crowfaq.html

www.jcrows.com/crowfct.htm

Jack Jouett's ride/Trevilians Station

http://www.ushistory.com/jjrguide.htm

http://www.ushistory.com/jouett.htm

http://www.americanrevolution.org/
jouett.html

www.louisacounty.com/jouett.htm

www.charlottesvilletourism.org/php-bin/
resource.php?id=781

www.trevilianstation.org

Guam

www.visitguam.org

www.guam.navy.mil/

http://ns.gov.gu/

Molas

http://www.panart.com/mola_gallery.htm

http://park.org/SanBlasDeCuna/
   molas.html
http://quilting.about.com/library/weekly/
   aa072297.htm

(Sites available as of press time. Author and publisher have no control over material on these sites or links to other Web sites.)

From Sugar's Bookshelves

Costa Rica, Insight Guides, edited by
   Harvey Haber

Field Guide to the Mid-Atlantic, National
   Audubon Society

Hoot, Carl Hiaasen

Jack Jouett's Ride, written and illustrated
   by Gail E. Haley

Mola Techniques for Today's Quilters,
   Charlotte Patera

Sign with your Baby, Joseph Garcia

The Amulet of Komondor, Adam Osterweil

The Emerald City of Oz, Frank Baum

The Rinkitink in Oz, Frank Baum

Glossary

Boa: A long fluffy snakelike scarf that is made of feathers or other fabrics.

Chenille: A fuzzy fabric, with tufts sticking out.

Confederate soldiers: Those who fought for the South during the Civil War.

Dragoons: Heavily armed cavalrymen.

Fledge: Acquire feathers for flying.

Kid gloves: Gloves made of soft leather from a lamb or baby goat.

Molas: Artistic sculptures with cloth made by Kuna Indian women of Panama. Molas often decorate clothing or are used as wall hangings. See p. 178 for example.

Toucan: A colorful bird in South and Central America that eats mostly fruit. It has a large bill.

Union soldiers: Those who fought for the North during the Civil War.

Velvet (on antlers): Soft skin that covers and nourishes the development of deer's antlers.

Vultures: Large birds with often featherless heads that eat mostly carrion (dead things).

This is typical, colorful mola made by female Kuna Indians in the San Blas Islands off the coast of Panama. Molas are created through a reverse applique process. The artists cut through many layers of fabric to expose the different colors. Molas often have designs of birds, animals, lizards, fish or everyday objects.

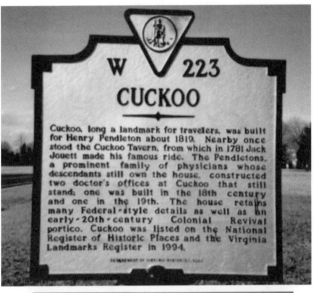

These signs are located at Cuckoo, the site of the old tavern, near Mineral, Virginia.

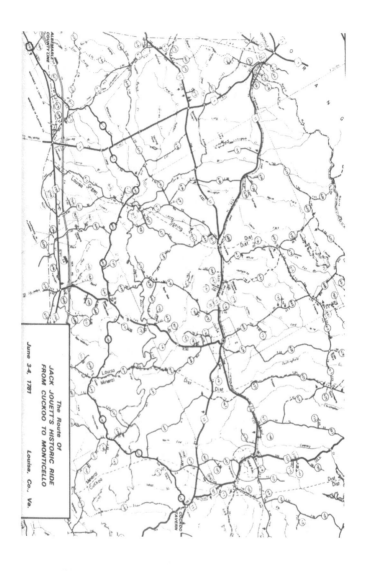

Map of Jack Jouett's ride from the tavern at Cuckoo
to Monticello courtesy of the Louisa County
Historical Society. Look for little circles to find the
route he took through Louisa County.

This version of the silhouette of Jack Jouett is courtesy of the Louisa County Historical Society. Before there were cameras and photography, silhouettes were created to show how people looked. They are cut from dark materials and fastened on a light background, or they are sketched and then filled in with dark ink or paint.

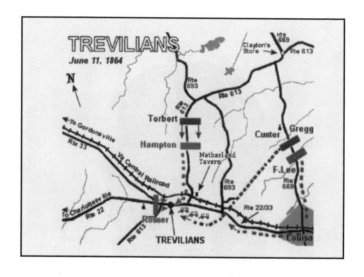

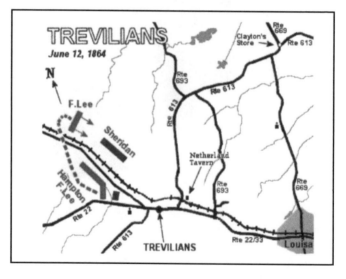

Maps of the two days of battles at Trevilians are courtesy the Trevilian Station Battlefield Foundation.

Photos from the 2004 reenactment of the Battle of Trevilian Station are courtesy of the Trevilian Station Battlefield Foundation. The top photo shows the Union calvary, and the lower one, the Confederates with a cannon on the smoky battlefield.

Acknowledgments

Many people have helped shape the *No Sisters Sisters Club* as they have read numerous drafts, helped with historical information or suggested slang that Bailey and her friends would use. Jim Salisbury; Nancy Miller, for the book club questions; Abigail Grotke; Julia Stallings; Natalie Wills and fourth-graders from Blessed Sacrament, Arlington, Virginia; Christopher Grotke, Pattie Cooke and the Louisa County Historical Society; Dr. Gaynelle Whitlock, president of the Mineral Historic Foundation; Kathy Stiles and the Trevilian Station Battlefield Foundation; Hallie Vaughan; Pam Gastineau, Lola Casy; Birdie Knoy; Muriel Van Patten; and Amber Freidel.

About the Author

Linda Salisbury draws her inspiration for the Bailey Fish series from her experiences in Florida and Central Virginia, and as a mother, mentor, former foster mother and grandmother.

She is a former newspaper editor and columnist, writes children's book reviews and articles for various publications. She is the author of five other books.

She enjoys boating on Lake Anna with her husband, Jim. They share their home with six lazy cats.

About the Artist

 Artist Christopher Grotke of Brattleboro, Vermont, is the creative director for MuseArts,Inc. He is an award-winning animator and has been featured in a number of publications, including the *Washington Post* and *New York Times,* and his work has been seen on PBS's "The Creative Spirit." Visit his Web site at www.musearts.com.

He has done illustrations and drawings for seven books. He has one adventurous cat, who likes to hike in the woods with him.